Trevor was born in North Staffordshire where he has lived all his life, is married with one daughter. He began his working career as a business management trainee with Michelin Tyres, a well-respected company in the local community.

Following that, he moved to the world famous Wedgwood Pottery employed within their finance department. A further career move secured him a management position within the Finance team of the local NHS. When Ilse and Trevor met at work, they shared the same ambition to write a book and decided to join forces to produce a manuscript.

Ilse was born in Chester and raised in a small village in rural Cheshire. One of a family of three girls, she was educated at the local High School. Her first job after leaving school was as a payroll clerk in Winsford. After a career move into the public sector in 1987, she began training as an accountant in the NHS.

Five years later, she moved to a job in North Staffordshire, where a promotional move located her in the same office as Trevor.

With similar ambitions as Trevor around creative writing and reading, the combination of the two authors provided the necessary ideas for the trilogy about Tommy.

THE THING
ABOUT TOMMY

Trevor Pettitt & Ilse Newsome

The Thing About Tommy

NIGHTINGALE BOOKS

NIGHTINGALE BOOKS

A CIP catalogue record for this title is
available from the British Library
ISBN 1 903491 16 9

*Nightingale Books is an imprint of
Pegasus Elliot MacKenzie Publishers Ltd.*
www.pegasuspublishers.com

First Published in 2003

**Nightingale Books
Sheraton House Castle Park
Cambridge England**

Printed & Bound in Great Britain

Dedication

Ilse & Trevor wish
to dedicate this book
to their parents.

Chapter 1

"Thomas Ravensdale. Will you be kind enough to join us?" Tommy jumped as the ruler slammed down hard against the desk, so close to his fingers. Suddenly he was back in the real world. Miss Tonge was livid, her hairy nostrils flared as she vented her frustration upon him. She continued screeching in her high, shrill nasal voice.

"What exactly is it that you find so interesting out of that window?" Without waiting for an answer, she snorted. "All that I can see is the sports field and the bicycle shed. Oh I see, so that's what it is. You want to waste your life on daydreaming all day? Well let me tell you..." Tommy stopped listening again. He had no interest in Miss Tonge's ranting or in the fact that the diameter of a circle is equal to square pies (whatever they are), or something like that...

This was not the first time he had experienced serious confrontation from Miss Tonge about daydreaming. She seemed so vexed about his happy little world, where to him life was suited to children without any influence from 'grown-ups' to spoil a perfect existence. Tommy's eyes glazed again, some power beyond the physical drawing him into another experience. It was another world, one without school, parents or teachers and horrid medicines. A world where children were always children, where a vivid imagination became reality and dreaming was not frowned upon.

"Tommy – Thomas! Have you not heard me? Pay

attention." As he turned his head, his blond, curly hair flopped into his blue eyes and he looked at the floor. He had developed this strategy as a defence against adults: it looked submissive, and if he looked at the floor for long enough, they soon ran out of steam. Anyway, he had far more important things about which to worry. Martha, his Dad David's new wife had invited him to stay for the half-term week. On the face of it that seemed like such a good idea. He would get to spend the week with Dad, but then he would have to share his Dad, not only with Martha and her prissy ways, but Clarissa. Now Clarissa had to be the most spoiled child in the history of the world. Tommy was always tempted to pull her long spiteful ginger plaits every time he met her. He never had… yet…

Suddenly Tommy realised that Miss Tonge was still speaking.

"And what is more, your father is coming to collect you, or so I believe…" she turned her back and stalked to the front of the classroom. Tommy could feel the rest of the class smirking, not at him, but purely because they were escaping the full wrath of Miss Tonge. He watched Miss Tonge as she walked to the teacher's desk. She was so regimented, with her grey flannel suit, burgundy shirt and severe haircut, he could not contemplate her ever enjoying herself. He often compared Miss Tonge to the most hideous of creatures either real or mythical. Her spotty face, her pointed nose (or beak as others referred to it) and discoloured teeth conjured up a remarkable resemblance to a gorgon. A hideous mythological beast with snakes for hair and the ability to turn people into stone with one glare. Yes, that was about the size of it – a perfect description, he thought.

Teachers, he decided, where probably the most boring people in the history of the whole wide world and he hoped he would never grow up to be like Miss Tonge. Tommy realised that she was still screeching: "I shall have great pleasure in informing him of your laziness and tardiness." This concerned Tommy slightly, he knew he was not lazy, but he was sure he did not even begin to know what 'tardiness' was. It sounded like an adult thing.

Whilst he contemplated Miss Tonge's verbal abuse, he could feel his neck and ears beginning to flush. He was not immune to humiliation and this had to be it. Why did she have to pick on him? There were other more abusive children in the class, but Miss Tonge insisted on picking on him.

Oh how he wished she was in his world, then things would be completely different. He could just 'think' her quiet and a great big piece of sticking plaster would firmly fix itself across her mouth, denying her the power of speech. Oh what a delightful thought!

He drew breath to defend himself and immediately the 'end of school bell' rang, much to the appreciation of the rest of the class. Miss Tonge was undeterred.

"Will you sit down, you unruly class? I will not have behaviour like this."

Everyone pretended to sit down, but was perched on the edge of their seats. Miss Tonge, as ever, waited until everyone was quiet, purely as an exercise in mind-control. Then she shouted. "All right class, you may leave." There was a mad scramble for the door. Tommy slowly gathered his pencil case and books together; he was not convinced that this Friday afternoon was altogether a good thing. He had no desire to be subjected to the torture of his Dad's new wife, or for that matter her awful, awful daughter – Clarissa. There was nothing more to be said. This was going to be hard work. For a start they were both girls, for heaven's sake, and they lived in a far better house than him and Mum.

Head bowed, trudging slowly to the door, he thought he had escaped when.

"Tommy." The shriek was like a banshee. "You stay behind." His heart sank. This was definitely not going to be his day. "I want to have a little chat with your father. We will sit and wait for him together." Tommy turned, still looking at the floor and dragged his feet back to the closest desk to the door. He sat down with a thud and sighed heavily. Miss Tonge drew her chair up to the other side of the desk. Tommy was sure he had never felt quite so intimidated, and then she began to speak again in a more reasonable voice.

"Tommy, what is it? You're not a naughty or disruptive boy by nature. I know that. However just recently, you don't seem to want to learn and I have to find out why. You're an intelligent boy. Whatever is it that is wrong?" she lowered her voice and asked softly. "Is everything all right at home?" Tommy did not want to engage in conversation, this sudden burst of 'niceness' was not characteristic of Miss Tonge.

What on earth had possessed her to ask that? What on earth could he say? Of course things were not all right at home, they had never been more wrong. How could she begin to understand? Yet it was none of her business what Tommy did at home. To Tommy's immense relief, the classroom door opened and in walked David, his father. Tommy leapt to his feet.

"Dad!" he exclaimed. "You're late. Are we going?" By this time, Tommy was halfway through the door and his father had to grab him and direct him gently back into Miss Tonge's dreaded lair.

"Hold on there, mate," he ushered Tommy back to his chair. "Miss Tonge wants to have a bit of a chat first," he turned to Miss Tonge, who seemed to have grown in

14

stature and was smiling most unnervingly. "So what seems to be the trouble Miss Tonge? What is it that Tommy has done exactly?" Miss Tonge drew breath and Tommy could not believe the words that came out of her mouth.

"Well," she began triumphantly, "it's more a case of what he has not done really." Tommy's mouth fell open. Here she was, having picked on him for ages and now she was grassing him up to his own father. "Tommy is an intelligent boy, and I do not want to see him wasting his time and throwing away his potential career." Tommy's father drew a breath either to ask a question, or to respond to this sudden onslaught, but Miss Tonge went on. She was gaining momentum now.

"I have a feeling that Tommy's problems either stem from troubles he is having at home or those he has created himself. Are things settled there Mr Ravensdale?" she continued immediately, without drawing breath or waiting for a response. "Or what I believe to be his main trouble are his friends. Now I believe Tommy is either being led astray, or being bullied by the most obnoxious, unruly boys in the school. So," she turned to Tommy, who drew away from her in horror. Now she was going to humiliate him further. Was there to be no end to this? "Tommy!" She was getting more and more high pitched now. "Which is it to be Tommy? We can only help you if you are prepared to help us. Are you being bullied?" Tommy suddenly realised his mouth was opening and closing, yet no sound was coming from him. What on earth could he say to that? True. The boys, to whom she had referred, had befriended him at the start of the year. Yet they had soon started taking his dinner money off him and now he avoided them like the plague, but that had nothing to do with this. His problem in Miss Tonge's class was pure and simple. It was Miss Tonge!

At last, Mr Ravensdale spotted an opportunity to respond and make a break for the door. At the same time he gathered Tommy and his books in one swift movement and edged his way out into the corridor.

"Well," he said, with a distinctly false smile. "Thank you so much for drawing my attention to this matter. Tommy and I obviously need to talk about this with his mother before we decide what to do about it. However, with respect Miss Tonge, Tommy does daydream a great deal, like most children his age. I would have thought you would understand but perhaps it's a long time since your mind wandered into another dimension. Tommy tells me sometimes about his dreams. They are quite vivid actually. Perhaps you should ask him to explain them to you one day."

'Go on Dad. Tell her.' He muttered under his breath. Tommy perked up now, he knew Dad would come round to his side, but he sensed that his father was none too pleased with this latest confrontation. There would be hell to pay later, he thought.

With that, he grabbed hold of the back of Tommy's blazer and the two of them left the school premises in thirty seconds flat.

Miss Tonge stood with her mouth open. She had not expected Mr Ravensdale to respond in such a manner. 'I am not wrong.' She thought 'He is!' Teachers are never wrong though are they?

Tommy's father had not spoken since they left the classroom. As they approached the car, Tommy's heart sank again as he saw Clarissa sitting haughtily in the back seat with a grin on her face. He groaned, contemplating the week before him and wondering what Dad would tell his mother next time he saw her.

"Get in right now," snapped his father, which he

quietly did, expecting him to get straight in and drive away.

The door slammed and Tommy instinctively reached for his seat belt.

"OK," said Mr Ravensdale, and Tommy became aware that his father was not driving away. His voice had softened, but was still firm. "Do you want to tell me what all that was about young man?" Tommy shook his head slowly. Firstly, he was not sure he knew the answer himself and secondly, he was damned sure he did not want to talk about it in front of old freckle-face. "We will talk when we get home." Mr Ravensdale turned around and they drove for nearly fifty minutes in absolute silence.

Chapter 2

As the car motored on, Tommy ignored Clarissa sitting bolt upright in the back seat. Yet somehow she managed to raise the hairs on the back of his neck.

"Hello, Tommy's in trouble again!" He failed to respond and decided a code of silence would be his best bet. Minutes later his dream world began to take over his imagination again. This time, he found himself riding the cosmic winds on his skateboard with the skill of an Olympic Champion. A few nose-grinds, nollies, and one hundred and eighty degree turns proved that he was a champion amongst fellow skateboarders. He had the stars above him, the earth beneath him and the wind at his back. What more could he want? Certainly, he did not want or need Miss Tonge hassling him. Suddenly he was aware that they were arriving at their destination. His imaginary dream world was gradually fading away, away. Until;

The car pulled into the huge driveway. Tommy looked up at the grand old house: it was exactly as his Dad had described it to him. Apparently it had been in Martha's family for hundreds of years and Clarissa had told him that it had been put on some special listing somewhere. It was a peculiar looking house. Obviously it had been very grand at some point, but a prominent feature were the twelve steps up to the front door. How did he know that? It was a thought that had just popped into his head. As they came to a standstill he quickly counted the steps: 'ten, eleven, twelve.' There were twelve, that was strange! What happened next was even stranger. Tommy froze as he put his foot on the first step, his eyes fixed firmly on the front door. Mr Ravensdale had driven the car away to the garage and Clarissa had made her way up the steps as Tommy flipped back into his other world.

This time he immediately sensed danger. This was not familiar to him. He felt scared, alone and in circumstances beyond his control. The mood seemed like a jigsaw puzzle, all falling into place and the last piece fitting into its rightful position. Tommy was in a place of semi-darkness, it was cold and musty, the smell was putrid and Tommy could feel the panic rising within him. His eyes began to glaze over and his legs began to wobble. This was not the place of comfort and tranquillity he was used to. It seemed the beginning of a nightmare.

"Tommy? Tommy, are you all right?" Tommy felt a pat on his back and this represented a return to a normal world with which he was familiar. A sudden jerk and startled yelp reunited him with normality and the look in his eyes alerted his father to Tommy's plight.

"Yes, I'm OK Dad. I just felt a bit funny when I started to climb the steps." Seconds later he felt like his old self again and the experience had passed. They both cleared the steps to the door and before Mr Ravensdale could fit the key in the lock, the heavy piece of oak began to swing open. They all looked to see who would greet them, but no one was there!

Those few seconds seemed like an eternity. The familiar warning signs should have alerted Tommy to potential danger. However, his young age and inexperience to the big wide world dampened them. Why were the hairs on the back of his neck standing up on end? Why was there a chilly breeze that came from inside the house, and why had all his senses put him on alert?

Suddenly Martha stood in front of them. Where had she come from? Tommy was sure she had not been there a few seconds before.

"Tommy, this is Martha. You do remember her don't you?" Tommy shrugged his shoulders; the feeling of panic began to subside slightly.

"Of course I do Dad. Do you think I'm stupid?"

"Just checking! For a minute there you looked as if you were in another world. Although that's not unusual for my little man now, is it?" Those words infuriated him. True, Mums and Dads have their pet names for their kids, but not at his age and especially not in front of Clarissa. He could just hear her repeating those awful words, 'Little Man'. This week had the makings of a complete and total disaster.

"Hello Tommy! Welcome to our new home. We hope you like it, it's far more interesting than the lodge we were in before. Now we have the opportunity to expand and be a part of the local history as the family was before." These were strange words to an eleven year old. All that Tommy knew was that Martha had stolen his Dad and left his mother and himself without a husband or a father. That was inevitable though. The family atmosphere had got progressively worse over a twelve-month period. Dad had his new job that took him all over Europe and was never at home, sometimes for months at a time, and family life seemed to disappear. Tommy and his mother had both been leading a life without the presence of a father and husband for as long as Tommy could dare to remember.

The arguments that ensued were volatile and at times quite vociferous. Many times both he and his mother were in tears as a result of the shouting and arguing. Once it had become completely out of hand. A neighbour, in the next flat, had called the police out of concern for both his and his mother's safety. However, Tommy's father was not a violent person. He had never, ever hit Tommy and would never even think about it. It was just 'the heat of he moment' that had caused the scene. After that his mother and father drifted apart and finally decided to part company, the divorce followed within months. It was not long after that it had become apparent to Tommy that his father had met up with Martha. She seemed to have exactly the same temperament as his father (or so his mother had said) and they were both ideally suited for each other. Tommy was not sure how Martha had parted company with her husband, his father never talked about it and Tommy had never asked.

Tommy knew exactly what to expect from Martha. She seemed a very loving wife and mother. She loved to hug and kiss people and Tommy knew he would be no exception to this. 'Oh well,' he thought, 'Here we go.'

"...And it's lovely to see you again!" Martha grabbed hold of Tommy and hugged him until he was breathless. This was a ritual that would appear to happen every time they were to meet, but this time it was decidedly different.

The second her arms wrapped around him he had another most unusual experience.

There was a door directly in front of him, but it had no walls to hang from or into which it should fit. To Tommy it seemed the room was no longer a room: there was no floor and no ceiling, just a door arched at the top with a handle which glowed in the sudden eerie semi-darkness. The handle beckoned to Tommy and somehow it desperately needed to be opened. He reached for it, but it seemed to take an eternity and the closer he got the brighter it became. Three metres, two, one metre. By this time, the handle was almost incandescent. The handle was cool to the touch, and there appeared to be no apparent danger, no reason to prevent him from opening the door.

The door swung open immediately he touched the handle yet there was nothing there, just open semi-dark space. Suddenly he had a vision of falling, yet he was unable to stop and had no way of knowing where he would land. This was confusing: he knew he had passed through the doorway but where did it lead? Curiosity was still uppermost in his mind. Would his vision soon become a reality? As he fell, he turned head over heels. The experience was now becoming one of fear, especially for one so young, he was only eleven years old after all. Tommy tried to reassure himself by thinking that this situation was only make believe. He had been scared in this dream and somehow he knew that it was only an extension of his own imagination, although somehow this did appear to be most vivid and almost surreal.

All sense of time had disappeared and this twilight world into which he was so rapidly sinking, did not give any reference points for comfort. It also gave no indication of where he was, or where he appeared to be going.

Suddenly, through sensation rather than sight or touch, he stopped and began to retrace his journey back. He began to feel withdrawn from the journey through which he had already travelled, almost a 'déjà vu' scenario, but from back to front as it were, or should that be in reverse? The door in front of him closed and disappeared and then suddenly…

"Yes. It really is good to see you again Tommy." Martha released her grip and Tommy snapped back into real time. "Enjoy your stay at the Manor House. Clarissa will show you around, your bedroom is at the top of the stairs. It's the one with the grandfather clock outside."

Tommy showed no signs of disturbance from his recent visions and he attempted to take them in his stride.

This place was obviously very old and he decided that it had many different kinds of architecture inside and out, developed, in his opinion, over many, many years. Best to keep his mind occupied on things he understood rather than those he did not. He made a point of recognising the Victorian and Georgian windows and knowledgeably decided that there was definitely a hint of Tudor style around the front door. These were rational thoughts and he concluded that he had understood where they came from. His most recent history lessons at school had been about how to recognise when buildings had been constructed, what influences were placed on architecture and how to recognise the signs. The history lessons were clearly useful in this instance, otherwise what was the point of spending so much time at school?

Without any warning, Clarissa appeared on the scene. Her usual smirk paraded across her extremely smug and freckled face. 'Oh, this really had to be the pits or worse', Tommy thought to himself as he turned to greet her and managed to raise a half-hearted smile to this most heinous of creatures.

"Take Tommy to see his room Clarissa. His is the guest room at the top of the stairs." Like a dutiful daughter, Clarissa escorted Tommy up the stairs to the guest room. She eyed his small suitcase with immense distaste, but Tommy had packed it with everything he could possibly need for his brief visit to this house.

The ticking of the grandfather clock at the top of the stairs got louder as they approached. The stairs themselves were quite wide and galleried and the wood gave off a pungent smell of age and polish. It appeared to Tommy that the history of the house must have gone back for many hundreds of years. The sight of what was about to greet Tommy however must have been able to tell him much, much more about the history of the Manor House. The huge grandfather clock at the top of the stairs towered above him it stood at least two metres high. He stood and gazed in awe at the sight before him. Never before had he seen such a sight, a symbol of age and immense power. It was a guardian strong, powerful and a centurion of time. It was knocked and chipped by the ravages of age and yet it stood like a monument to the whole house, depicting a fearsome sight.

The face of the clock was the focal point, a face enough to put the fear of God into anyone, let alone a boy of his age. The 'face' was an appropriate description of what was before him, but this somehow oozed what could only be described as a feeling of uncertainty.

The face was made of what looked like brass and was square in shape. There were strange figures where the numbers should have been. Tommy knew what these were as he had learned about them at school. 'Roman numerals' they were called. He could not quite think why they weren't Roman numbers, but then everything that was very old was strange, especially to him.

The face of the clock seemed to leer at him in a strange and intimidating way that was integral to the whole piece. He stood directly in front of the clock and raised his head to determine the height of the entire piece and suddenly realised how tall it really was. There was something else compelling about this clock and he could feel it but could not define what it meant. Normally on a grandfather clock, Tommy thought, there were pictures and decoration around the face. Not this one however, it was quite plain in design. The most unusual thing about it was that there was no door in the front of the case. Every other large clock Tommy had seen had a door at the front for access to the pendulum. This clock must have some other method of access. Somehow the ticking was reverberating through his body, but not just because he was so close. He could feel some sort of connection or bonding with the clock. It could be the clock, or was it the house? Maybe it was both of them, but Tommy could not be sure right now.

"This is your room Tommy." Clarissa opened the huge mahogany door and to Tommy's surprise there was no noise, creak, squeak or otherwise. Tommy had anticipated some sort of nightmarish noise from the hinges, but there was just the ticking of the clock that stood like a sentinel, just outside the room. He sized up the room in just a few moments and it blended well with the character of the rest of the house. Wood-panelled walls, a huge fire place with architecture and a cornice that decorated every nook and cranny. There was a double bed, two wardrobes and three sets of drawers. However, there was no computer. 'Oh well,' he thought 'you can't win them all.'

The room felt comfortable, far more so than the rest of the house and anyway, he was only staying for a week and then he would be back with his mother. Oh how he wished his mother and father were still together. This Martha was OK, he supposed, but in all seriousness she was not his mother.

"See you later," Clarissa muttered. "Then I'll show you around the rest of the house."

"Yeah, OK," replied Tommy. His reluctance was obvious in his response, however he did not want to be the one who would spoil the few precious days with his Dad.

There had been the faint promise of a Halloween party, which both he and Clarissa would attend together with a few of Clarissa's friends. A couple of day trips had also been promised to surprise destinations and rumour was that one day would be a trip to Alton Towers. It had all sounded great, all that quality time he would get to spend with his Dad. However, he could not help thinking that maybe he and Mum would never have parted if there had been similar events then… but at least now he had his Dad.

Tommy began unpacking his clothes methodically. He was actually quite a tidy person for a boy of his age. Mechanically, he placed his socks and underwear in the drawers, hung up his shirts on coat hangers and placed his toiletries in the en-suite room. Next to his toothbrush were his body spray and after-shave. Although he was only eleven, he had tried shaving once and ended up with a large plaster on his chin. He had bought after-shave for the big 'S' day and he supposed he would on this day become a man. Last of all to unpack was his picture of Mum and Dad, something he treasured amongst all his other possessions. This would have pride of place on the dresser unit by the wall. On the other side of the wall rested the grandfather clock and, if he listened quietly, he could still hear it ticking.

Tommy approached the dresser with his picture and somehow each step he took towards the wall seemed to have meaning. It was as if someone was pushing him from behind – no, it was as if the clock was pulling him. He could not tell and it took a serious amount of concentration to place the picture in the centre of the unit. He took a long time measuring the centre point and manoeuvring it to oversee where he would sleep. Unintentionally, he touched the wall and suddenly he felt a cool breeze that appeared to come from nowhere and travel directly through his body. Suddenly a vision of the door appeared again, still with the strange glow around the edge. Again, he wondered how the door managed to remain upright with no walls or support. He questioned himself. What was its purpose? It appeared so menacing and mysterious yet inviting to an inquisitive mind. He must exercise extreme caution if he was to consider further investigation.

Again Tommy began to approach the strange apparition. There was no knowing what lay beyond the bare structure but he knew he had to find out and its initial threatening appearance had been subsumed by his overall inquisitiveness.

Chapter 3

"Tommy. Tommy." The door of the bedroom burst open and Clarissa appeared. "Are you ready for your guided tour of the house? I did promise you." Tommy's vision again disappeared as quickly as it had arisen.

"Erm. Oh. What?" he regained normality, removing his hand from the wall. "Yeah, sure. Now?"

"Well only if you want to. You don't sound too keen now!" Clarissa's face signalled a change of mood at the potential rejection of her personal company and no bag of sweets would be sufficient to retrieve the situation. Tommy realised this, but played a cool game and he uttered words to pacify her.

"We shall start in your bedroom then. As far as Mummy can determine, the appearance of this room has not been altered in centuries and is one of the oldest parts of the original house. It dates back to at least medieval times about 1300 AD, but she suspects that it goes back even further than that. During the history of the house, it has had many parts added and either all or some of those parts have been destroyed at sometime by fire or some other awful event. During the Second World War, a bomb hit the stables on the outside of the Manor House, demolishing the stables and blowing out all of the windows on the east side. Part of the roof disappeared and the chimney-stack crashed through the roof and attic killing one of the servants in the house. After that, most of the land was sold off for housing, only the Manor House and the lodge remained in the existing grounds.

"Back during the First World War a German family with British nationality worked as servants in the Manor House. They worked very hard, however records show that they would not be drawn into the conflict and became conscientious objectors. That apparently sealed their fate and a bomb was placed in the servants' quarters downstairs, it went off killing them both and another maid. The murderers were never caught. After that Mummy's family could not afford to manage the whole house and they moved into the lodge next door and lived there for many years. The Old Manor was empty for decades and fell into disrepair. They had it boarded up for security and was never occupied until several years ago when Mummy decided to restore it to its former glory."

Clarissa seemed quite bright and well informed of the history of the house, Tommy thought. They both now had wandered onto the galleried landing and she pointed out the other bedrooms. This one was hers, positioned next door to Tommy's. It was tastefully decorated for a young girl with all the mod cons associated with comfortable, modern living. Next to Clarissa's bedroom was his Dad's and Martha's, then a fourth and fifth that required some renovation. They climbed a flight of stairs into the attic, which served as a dumping ground for all those possessions acquired that do not have a place in the living area of the house. Clarissa pointed out to Tommy the old relics that had been left there by previous owners and not been afforded review by the current occupants.

"Someday, Mummy said she would try to go through all of these boxes. I said that they were horrid and dirty and that David should clear them out." Tommy realised that Clarissa had referred to his Dad as 'David', and not as he would have expected, 'Mr Ravensdale'. He frowned at her familiarity but decided that he would have to just get used to it. They both returned to the floor below and the next room she pointed to was the bathroom. It was by far the most spacious Tommy had ever seen and it even had two baths! However bathrooms are not at the leading edge of interest to eleven year old boys. Tommy was not an exception to the rule.

There was a second set of stairs next to the bathroom leading to the ground floor. The two children walked down them next to one another. Clarissa continued the commentary about the Manor House. She explained that these stairs were another part of the old house and used to be the only stairs in the building. The other stairway and galleried landing had been added later. He could tell from the treads that the wood was very old and rickety. People in the house would be able to hear anyone climbing these stairs, they made such a racket. This had to be a far better device than an ordinary alarm system in case of burglars.

They emerged by another mysterious looking door with a plate headed up 'Cellar'. Tommy went to open the door, whereupon Clarissa immediately stopped him.

"No!" she barked. "We do not go down there! It's too dangerous. Mummy says so. I have never been down there."

"Oh!" said Tommy. "Don't you ever wonder? Have you never wanted to investigate? Have you never been curious?"

"Well… Yes, at times, but it always seems very scary. Once Mummy went down there and a few minutes later I heard her scream. She came running up the stairs and looked really frightened."

"What happened then?"

"Well, I think when she saw me, she tried not to look so frightened and appeared that everything was normal – however – I don't really know. Come on, I'll show you the rest of the house."

Reluctantly he accompanied Clarissa, turning as they moved away from the cellar door and wondering just what was behind that door. The ground floor consisted of an enormous living room with a large screen television that must have been the size of a chest freezer, well almost. Tommy hadn't spotted Martha and David at the far side of the room, but Clarissa had.

"Hi Mummy. I am just showing Tommy around the house."

"Oh thank you darling, but make sure you do not go down into the cellar, you know it's dangerous."

"I've already explained that to him…"

David interrupted. "Yes Tommy, do not go down there. It needs a great deal of renovation and we've not had chance to arrange it yet. The place could be very dangerous."

"OK Dad," Tommy responded, but never followed up with the hundreds of questions now forming in his mind. Turning to Clarissa he muttered. "Let's go." They continued the tour of the house, but somewhere deep in the back of his mind was the thought of the cellar! The remainder of the ground floor included another day room, a dining room with a table big enough to dance upon. There was a kitchen, laundry room and so on and it seemed to go on for ever. By this time Tommy was becoming bored with the tour, a room here, another room there. They were all starting to look the same to him – all except for the door to the cellar.

The last room was called 'the morning room' as Clarissa announced so proudly. Her words were almost snooty, just like that snooty 'Patsy' at his school. To Tommy it was just another room in a long list of boring rooms. He grabbed the brass handle to open the door, then instantly before him appeared the suspended door again. All fear and apprehension had suddenly disappeared and curiosity now seemed to be the dominant factor. He marched toward the illuminated handle of the suspended door with its wooden arch and iron fixtures, his hand outstretched. He looked around for Clarissa but she was nowhere in sight. 'Good,' he thought. He had to find out what was behind that door, it was becoming almost a test of his boyhood curiosity, but it had to be satisfied.

Tommy grabbed the handle and the glow transmitted itself through his body. He began to feel most peculiar. He did not feel threatened or in any danger, but confident and strong and determined to discover the contents of the room that must surely lie behind the door. The door mechanism clicked with precision, releasing its hold on an imaginary door frame. It swung open and Tommy was sucked again into a different world. The darkness showed no sign of revealing its secrets and everywhere he looked was pitch black. Except for a small spot of light above him and one below him, the spot below him was gradually getting larger as he floated towards it and steadily he began to experience a fall.

"Tommy, Tommy. Tommy! Are you daydreaming again?" The familiar, piercing voice of Clarissa seemed to suck him back toward the door. In an instant he was back to reality, with his hand on the brass door handle.

"Are you going to open that door or not?" he turned the handle and the door swung open.

The room looked as if it had been dragged from the medieval era, a huge open fireplace took pride of place at the far side. It reminded him of his history books, but appeared more sinister as he gazed around. Coincidentally the room happened to be directly below Tommy's bedroom and the tick of the great grandfather clock at the top of the staircase echoed through the room. Clarissa explained that this was another room that required major renovation and also formed part of the original house.

"How old is the Manor House?" enquired Tommy.

"I am not very sure. Mummy has determined that it pre-dates the thirteenth century but how much farther back it goes, no one knows. The fireplace is inscribed 16th August 1193, during the reign of Richard the First. Although no one has authenticated it yet, I am sure that they will. One day Mummy is going to try and discover he full history from the library in the village. Apparently they have loads of records going right back to when the house was first built."

"Oh," replied Tommy. "I would like to help with that, shall we both go to the library tomorrow and see if we can find anything?"

Clarissa was surprised at Tommy's offer. She knew he had a tendency to be distant and had never before contemplated playing or let alone working together.

"OK. I will tell Mummy that we are going into the village tomorrow. She may give us a lift." The pact was made, they needed confirmation from both parents, but that seemed to be purely academic.

Chapter 4

Outside the house were well-laid flower beds and cultivated lawns. The land on which the Manor House stood was only a fraction of what it had once been, although it was still sufficient to infer it's grandeur and status within the locality.

The tour was over and it was time to eat. It was getting dark outside and the mystery of the Manor House began slowly to close in those within.

"Would you like some more potatoes Tommy?" Martha asked.

"No, thank you. I have had enough now."

"How did the tour go?" his father asked.

"Oh, OK I suppose."

"You don't like our new house Tommy? It's far better than the lodge and it's certainly far more spacious." What Tommy did not want to openly admit was that he missed his Mum and Dad living together. Whether it was in the Manor House or in any old flat, they just had to be together.

"Why don't both of you catch an early night tonight and then the rest of the week you can stay up late?"

"How late Dad?" Tommy was clearly in negotiating mood.

"Oh, what do you think Martha?"

"Well, if you've both behaved then shall we say eleven to eleven-thirty?"

"Oh yes! Thanks Martha."

"Thank you Mummy," replied Clarissa. With that

huge concession given by the grown ups they both kissed Martha and David goodnight and retired to bed.

"Gracious," said David. "What could have happened? At one time they could not stand the sight of one another and now they are talking as if they're the best of buddies."

Martha responded. "It's this house. For the last few weeks there have been several very minor events that I've noticed that may be regarded as strange. It's never happened before. Or if it has, I haven't realised it."

"Sounds like this house has more to offer than shelter. Someday it may reveal it's inner most secrets," he replied.

Tommy returned to the living room and most apologetically asked for a glass of water to take to bed. Martha smiled and obliged him by filling a pint glass with fresh spring water.

"Now off to bed Tommy," she urged him. He thanked her and made his way to the stairs.

The galleried stairs were quiet and a little scary as he ascended. His attention was focused on the enormous grandfather clock at the top. Step by step he drew nearer just as it began to strike nine o'clock. Five, six, seven, eight, nine and now he was a mere metre from the clock.

'That clock is pretty scary,' he thought, passing by it to his bedroom. Once inside he washed, brushed his teeth and put on his pyjamas, but it was still only nine thirty and he was wide awake. 'I know Dad said have an early night but I'm not at all tired.' Tommy lay in bed and played for a while on his Gameboy and the next time he checked his watch it was nearly twelve midnight. 'Gosh,' he thought 'That went quickly.' Then he began to notice the ticking of the clock again.

He threw back his duvet and opened the bedroom door as the clock began to strike midnight. Eight, nine, ten, he counted, eleven but no twelve! By this time he was on the landing again, checking that there were no adults looking. He turned to the clock.

Tommy looked directly at the clock face. Again the suspended door appeared and he moved toward it once more, determined to solve this mystery. He passed quietly though the doorway and this time found himself in a tunnel of darkness. Then a pinpoint of light appeared in the distance and he turned towards it, his fear quickly disappearing. The light increased in size as time passed. Strange though, he could not see the face of his wrist watch, he had no idea how much time had passed. Where was this leading? Was it a dream or reality? His Mum would go wild if she knew what he was doing – mostly at his Dad though, for allowing it to happen.

Once again he was subjected to a falling sensation which stopped suddenly as he settled in front of a second door. He knew this was not the same door through which he had entered and anyway this one opened inwards and not outwards. It took several seconds for him to summon up the courage to open the door, but it was his inquisitiveness that got the better of him: it needed an answer to all of this. The door mechanism clicked with precision to release it from its jamb. He pulled it toward him, still a little apprehensive of what could be on the other side.

Fully open, the sight before him was astonishing. He had somehow landed in the middle of his last lesson this afternoon. Heaven forbid. He was back in Miss Tonge's class!

Tommy woke with a start. 'What was that noise?' He was sure he had heard something. He realised that the covers were still over his head. Why had he still got the covers over his head? Slowly, the events of the previous night began to replay themselves in his head. He had actually gone through the door this time, and where had it taken him but to a replay of an awful Friday afternoon nightmare with Miss Tonge.

Realising that it was now daylight and sun was streaming through the crack in the curtains Tommy leapt out of bed. As he grabbed his clothes and dashed for the bathroom, he glanced at the clock. Eight thirty-two! That was quite late for him. He did not normally sleep so late.

Tommy dashed in and out of the shower as fast as he could. He had to tell his Dad about this adventure. As he flew down the stairs, he could hear familiar breakfast sounds emanating from the kitchen.

"Dad!" he yelled breathlessly. His father stopped in mid-sentence.

"Tommy. What have I told you about interrupting grown-ups when they are speaking?" Clarissa paused with a spoon of cereal halfway to her mouth. This had got to be good.

"But Dad…"

His father snapped back. "No. Don't but… I am talking and I am in a hurry." Both he and Martha left through the door to the hallway. Tommy's mouth was still open, ready to protest again, but instead he sighed in exasperation and shrugged his shoulders.

"What's up Shorty?" Clarissa had put down her spoon and was eyeing Tommy curiously. Tommy sighed again. The urgency to tell someone was greater than the risk of Clarissa making endless fun of him. He sat opposite her at the table.

"Well," he began slowly.

"Get on with it," Clarissa snapped. "Tiffany's coming over and we're going into town to buy something to wear for the Pony Club disco. We can go to the library some other time." Tommy paused, he longed to pick up on that snippet of information, he was sure he would be able to use it to his benefit. However, his desperation to share his experience was too great.

"Last night," he began again. Clarissa nodded with encouragement "I went through the door!"

"What door?" Clarissa looked perplexed.

"Well there's this suspended door that appears from time to time and last night I went through it," he paused, waiting for the squeal of laughter, but none came.

"Where did it go?"

Tommy thought she had to be joking and answered carefully. "Well it must have been a dream, because I ended up at school yesterday afternoon."

Clarissa pulled a face. "Sounds more like a nightmare to me." Strangely she was taking him seriously.

"Clarissa," Tommy cringed as he said it, he never normally used her proper name, and he usually referred to her as 'She or Her'. "Is there something weird about this house?"

Clarissa looked at the floor. "How do you mean?"

"Well, you don't seem very surprised that something's happening."

"Do you have to start every single sentence with the word 'well'?"

Tommy opened his mouth to snipe back at her, then changed his mind, as he was about to start the insult with the very same word. Clarissa went on and shrugged her shoulders. "When Mummy and I first moved here, she did mention that the house had 'history' with our family and one day, she said she was going to research it properly. I don't think she's got around to it yet though."

Tommy considered this for a while. "Where was she going to research it from?" he asked, desperately trying not to start his sentence with the dreaded word.

Clarissa shrugged her shoulders again. "The library I suppose just like I told you yesterday, or weren't you listening?" The doorbell rang and interrupted them.

"Here's Tiff," she cried, bolting toward the door. She shouted back over her shoulder. "Tell you what Shorty. If you like, Mummy can drop us all off at the library. The shops are only a few minutes away and it solves your Dad's problem about what to do with you today."

Tommy trotted after her. "What do you mean?"

Clarissa paused Martha had already reached the front door. "Well, he has been called into work."

Tommy stopped dead in his tracks. He hadn't expected that. He was so stunned he didn't even pick Clarissa up on her use of that confounded word. At this point his father stuck his head around the living-room door-post.

"Sorry son," he said, looking sheepish. "I didn't know how to tell you."

Now, on the one hand this was the end of the world. On his own with Martha all day, that was certainly not good. For once, though, Clarissa had a good point – although he did not want to admit that right now. An idea began to form in his mind and the more he thought about it, the better it seemed.

"It's OK Dad," he said, trying not to sound even slightly pleased. "I'll go to the library instead." There was a sudden silence in the hallway. Tiffany, who was a look-alike for Clarissa, only with darker hair, stopped in her tracks as she rushed down the hall towards her friend and everyone turned to look at him.

"What?" his father looked stunned.

Tommy couldn't help himself: "Don't you mean pardon?"

They all had to laugh. It was true enough that Tommy

was always being corrected for that one.

"If you're sure…?" His father said hesitantly, trying not to show the relief he was feeling. Tommy nodded.

"We could drop him off Mummy," said Clarissa.

"Well, it certainly seems as if you have sorted that out between you," Martha said decisively. Tommy and Clarissa both grinned at each other, now even Martha was using the dreaded word. "Let's go," she picked up her keys and they all set off to their respective vehicles. Tommy, Clarissa, Martha and Tiffany to the green Range Rover and Tommy's father to his blue BMW. Tommy looked back and waved as both vehicles went in different directions at the bottom of the driveway.

"So, Thomas," announced Tiffany in a piercing voice. "What is it exactly that you feel the need to study?" Tommy turned his head away from them and stared out of the window.

"Don't Tiff. Leave him alone." Tommy could not believe what he was hearing. Had 'she' just been siding with him? Both he and Tiff stared at Clarissa, who went ever so slightly pink. "Well…" she started and both she and Tommy burst out laughing. Tiffany folded her arms and glared out of the other window. She knew she had missed out on something there but she would eat spinach before she would ask what.

Chapter 5

A short while later, Martha drew up outside the library.

"You two girls can walk from here. It won't do you any harm. Tommy! I'll be back at exactly twelve noon and I expect all three of you to be here. No arguments!" She glared at Clarissa who was pulling yet another face.

They got out of the Range Rover and Martha pulled carefully away into the traffic.

"Meet you back here then?" quizzed Clarissa. Tommy nodded and turned toward the library. He could hear Tiffany muttering to Clarissa as they walked away down the street.

Tommy looked at the library building. It was an old, grand museum-ish building, quite weathered but well tended. He slowly climbed the seven steps to the front door. His mind wandered: why was it that he counted steps? He had no idea why, but they were just there, waiting to be counted. As he contemplated this, he suddenly felt something very cold brush past him. He jumped sideways and turned, but there was nothing there. The hair on the back of his neck stood on end. Surely it could not happen here as well?

Tommy realised that he had reached the top of the steps and was now standing with his arm outstretched and ready to grasp the handle of the main door. His reluctance to turn the handle was based upon his previous track record, but this time he was prepared for it. He could not recall climbing the steps in his eagerness for information, but his desire to move from this place drove him into the library. His hand rested on the door handle as he tensed in anticipation. Pulling on the handle he released the catch. Tommy opened his eyes to see the interior of the library.

Inside, the building was cool and smelled musty. Tommy stopped right inside the door to allow his eyes to become accustomed to the poor lighting. Slowly his pupils adjusted and revealed the wealth of knowledge before him from which he intended to discover the secrets of the Manor House. To his right was a reception desk made from a dark-stained oak-like panelling that matched the panels on the wall behind. At this desk sat a very prim and proper looking woman; she was very slim and well dressed. It occurred to Tommy that she could have been at least one hundred years old. The majority of the rest of the room in which he now stood was lined with huge panel-ended racks laden with thousands of books. Books of all kinds, sizes and ages were neatly squeezed into every available space. There must have been literally thousands of them.

In the centre of the room, there was a complete change from the old, threadbare carpet, the surface was like a dance hall floor and was the reading area. Highly polished wood, with wooden chairs and tables lined neatly across the width of the room. The thought did cross his mind that surely wooden chairs on wooden floors would make considerably more noise than on carpet and surely a library was not a place renowned for noise? However someone must have thought that it was a good idea, mustn't they?

Slowly he became aware that there was someone watching him. Without his realising, a small, thin old man had approached him and was standing less than two metres to his left. As he turned to face him, Tommy was startled, but the old man smiled and nodded.

"Yes," he said quietly. "You appear quite nervous. You came through the door as if a pack of wolves were at your heels." As he came closer, Tommy could see that he had very white hair and a long white beard. He tried not to stare at the beard. The only person he knew with a beard was his headmaster and he obviously did not count as a real person. This man reminded Tommy of a mad professor-type person, strangely dressed but with a smile that beamed kindness and consideration for all he befriended. Tommy warmed to the man instantly. He felt no threat from him and began to explain his strange visions quite openly.

"Well…" he started, not caring that he had started with 'the word'. "There was something out on the steps…" he turned and pointed toward the door. When he turned back, the old man was smiling sympathetically.

"Ah! The Something. I fear it may be on the move again." Tommy looked closely at him. It was almost as if he knew of an 'entity' known as 'The Something'. Tommy shook his head slightly. What a ridiculous notion, he had obviously misheard.

"Come, let me help you find the answer." The old man held out his hand to Tommy and gestured for him to follow.

"The answer? To what?"

The man continued to smile knowingly and nodded in acknowledgement. "That is why people come to the library, to find the answer to their quest." This made perfect sense and Tommy had to agree with that. He followed curiously to see where the man would take him.

In a quiet corner, there was a small door in the panelling. To those who looked, it appeared invisible but behind the door lay a mountain of secrets. For some inexplicable reason this door reminded him of the suspended door, yet there was no resemblance. Was there another library behind the suspended door, or something evil? He had to find out. Libraries were not like this where Tommy lived; this one was friendly and interesting. Quite probably it was the most interesting library Tommy had ever visited.

"My name's Tommy," he said, suddenly conscious of his manners.

The old man looked at him sagely. "Yes," he said. "That fits." The answer puzzled Tommy. "I'm Wilf." Tommy was sure that he meant he knew what Tommy's name was, but how could he? Wilf turned the handle and opened the door.

"Hello Wilf," Tommy announced, holding out his hand.

Wilf took it and shook it solemnly. "Hello Tommy." They turned and walked through the open door.

Tommy stood for a few seconds, taking in the sight that met him. There was a high, stained glass window that diffused the light, but also drew attention to the holes in Wilf's oversized greyish cardigan.

The room was lined with shelves containing the most curious collection of old-fashioned leather-bound books that Tommy had ever seen. Under the shelves, in the same wood panelling as in the part of the library they'd just left, were chests with long, thin drawers stretching for at least five or six feet each. Tommy drew breath to ask, but Wilf answered before he had spoken.

"Maps. Old, ancient, antique and modern. It appears to be every map ever drawn of this area."

"Wow!" said Tommy.

"Wow?" Wilf emulated the word. "What does that mean?"

Tommy gasped. "I'm sorry!"

'Manners,' Tommy thought, 'Don't forget your manners.'

"Gosh! That really is impressive Mr Wilf."

Wilf looked genuinely confused. "No. Really, what does that mean?"

Tommy looked closely at his face. How old was this man? Was he making fun of him? He decided to take the chance that he really didn't know. "It's what you say when you're dead impressed with something."

"Do you mean 'very' or 'really' impressed?"

"You're making fun of me."

"No. I am merely correcting your grammatical content." Tommy was convinced he really was that old! "Anyway," Wilf continued. He could tell that he had offended Tommy and tried to make amends. "My speech must sound old-fashioned to you."

Tommy took a deep breath. "I suppose you spend much of your time in the library with all of these books? There won't be many younger people that you have contact with." There was a pause. Tommy knew that his sentence was probably a grammatical nightmare, possibly inappropriate and more than likely offensive and he felt his face physically drop in despair of retrieving the situation. After what seemed like an eternity, Wilf smiled and Tommy let out a huge sigh of relief.

"I will not correct that for you. I am sure that you are well intentioned."

Tommy nodded vigorously. He grinned.

"Sorry! I'm always being told off for my grammar and manners. I don't mean to be rude."

Wilf nodded, his thin fingers touching gently at the tips.

"Let's get to work, there is no time like the present," he motioned for Tommy to sit at the large desk in the middle of the room and headed toward one of the chests of drawers. He was still speaking but Tommy could barely hear him, he was convinced he had heard something like 'Although there was quite a good time just before the dark-ages that I quite enjoyed'. Again Tommy was sure he had mis-heard. He really would have to try harder to be attentive.

Wilf returned with about half a dozen discoloured sheets of what looked like old wallpaper and tried to place them on the desk. The desk however was covered in all kinds of things, ranging from an ornate angle-poise lamp to a huge letter rack crammed with unopened mail. Tommy rushed to move some of the items.

"Just find a space for them over there," Wilf muttered, nodding toward another chest of drawers. Tommy eagerly grabbed an armful of items and moved to where Wilf had indicated. He stopped abruptly. The rest of the room was more crowded than the desk. There was nowhere to 'put' anything. Carefully Tommy placed everything in a very neat heap as close to the chest of drawers as possible and returned to the desk.

Wilf had spread the papers across the desk and was re-arranging them into some sort of pre-ordained order. He looked up at Tommy.

"Now then! I think it will be best if we start from the farthest back and then work our way forward." Tommy peered at the map at the top of the pile.

"What exactly are we looking for?" It occurred to Tommy that Wilf was making huge assumptions here. "I haven't told you what I'm looking for."

Wilf looked up, startled and Tommy involuntarily checked to see if the door was still open. To his relief, he could see that it was and he could just about see the main entrance if he moved forward slightly. Wilf smiled gently and nodded, from his position standing over the table he could see exactly what Tommy was doing. He began to roll up the maps slowly.

"Perhaps that's enough for today Tommy," he said sadly. "You make sure you come back as soon as you feel you can. There's very little time left and The Something is becoming a serious problem." Tommy had moved toward the open door, but he stopped at the second mention of The 'Something'. He turned, feeling safer as he stood with one foot on the threshold.

"You talk about it as if there is something..." Wilf nodded as Tommy ran out of words.

"Tommy, Thomas Ravensdale..." The hairs on the back of Tommy's neck stood on end. How on earth did he know his full name? He opened his mouth but no words came out and Wilf continued. "I have been waiting for you to help me with this quest and it is only you who can help. I wish you no harm. You must believe that." His eyes were of piercing blue and he held Tommy's gaze for what seemed like an eternity. Now all of his hair, not only that on his head, but on his arms and legs was standing on end. He noticed how the light in the room suddenly dimmed. A cloud, that's right, a cloud must have crossed in front of the sun. Tommy's eyes shot to the window, and yet it appeared that the sun still shone out there. Tommy looked back at Wilf, who sat slowly down at the desk. He seemed suddenly older, if that were at all possible and he looked at Tommy over his half-moon spectacles. He took them off and rubbed his eyes.

"You are quite correct, there is something and it has a tangible presence..." There was a loud bang as the door to the room slammed shut, almost knocking Tommy to the floor. Without thinking, he grabbed it with the intention of remonstrating with whoever had slammed it on him. As he opened the door, he began to feel sick. There was no one there, just a cold, damp feeling which enveloped him slowly like wet fingers of fog.

Wilf stood up and walked toward him.

"You see? The Something is on the move and we – you and I – have to stop it before it becomes too strong." Tommy gave in to his fear. Manners or not, he could not deal with this any more. He bolted across the floor of the main library and yanked at the main door. To his horror, it would not open and he struggled with it, the panic rising within him.

"Got to get out of here," he muttered in frustration. He could feel his legs beginning to give way and his hands began to shake.

"Allow me," Wilf said quietly, who had surprisingly joined him at the door. Tommy stepped back and as Wilf opened the door he continued gently. "Don't fear me Thomas, fear The Something. You must come back. You know it and I know it. You cannot leave this question unanswered." Tommy hesitated, curiosity almost getting the better of him, but then to his surprise, he saw Clarissa and Tiffany on the steps and he shot out to meet them at the top step.

"Thank goodness," he almost shouted. "Where have you been?"

Tiffany snorted. "It's only eleven. She wanted to see what you were doing. I can't think why," she looked at Clarissa for support. Tommy turned and gazed back into the library, but Wilf had disappeared. Where had he gone? Surely an old man like him could not move that quickly – he was real wasn't he?

"You OK, Shorty?" she asked. Tommy nodded, still looking for Wilf. He didn't feel OK, and he certainly didn't want to deal with Tiffany on top of everything else. He shot Tiffany a quick glance and Clarissa got the message and changed the subject, much to Tommy's relief.

"We had a very successful trip and found the outfits in the second shop we visited. So we thought we'd waste the rest of the time finding out what you've been up to. It looks like you've finished whatever it is you are doing. So you can be a gentleman and treat us to tea and scones at Emily's."

Chapter 6

Emily's was the best teashop in town. Tommy felt in his pockets and was relieved that he hadn't had to explain himself. He just hoped that he had enough cash to buy three of the most expensive cream teas in the Western Hemisphere. Clarissa led the way, with Tiffany crowing about how sophisticated they were in extracting expensive treats out of her little step brother. Tommy followed, half mentally counting what he could feel in his pockets and half trying to make some sort of sense of what had just happened to him.

Half an hour later, the three of them sat around a beautifully laden table consuming scones and tea. To Tommy's immense relief, Clarissa had slipped him a five-pound note whilst Tiffany had gone to powder her nose. This, to Tommy, was a most peculiar expression. How many years must it have been since girls did actually go and powder their noses? Why couldn't they just admit that they were going to the ladies? If he or one of his mates were going, they just went for a whiz. Girls, Tommy decided to himself, were most peculiar creatures.

"So," a high-pitched Tiffany directed at Tommy. "What exactly was it that you were doing in the library?" Tommy looked straight at Clarissa, who immediately looked out of the window.

"Quick," she said suddenly. "There's Mummy. We shouldn't keep her waiting." Grabbing her bag, she hurried toward the door. Tommy dashed to the waitress and paid the bill, leaving Tiffany sitting by herself. She gathered her belongings and followed the others to the door with a slightly puzzled expression on her face. This was most unlike Clarissa. She normally only had time for Tommy when she was extracting some sort of amusement out of him. Yet today, it was as if they were plotting or concealing something together.

"Hello you lot." Martha opened the back door of the Range Rover. "Well done. You're all back on time and it looks as if you've been getting along together as well. I'm proud of you." Tommy and Clarissa nodded and Tiffany folded her arms and sulked.

Back at the house, Tiffany and Clarissa closeted themselves upstairs to examine their purchases and Martha went into the kitchen to begin preparing lunch. Tommy followed her slowly. The house felt a little different to him somehow, yet he couldn't quite put a finger on what it was. He sat at the breakfast bar opposite Martha and absently began to shell the fresh garden peas she had placed by a bowl. Martha looked at him closely.

"Are you feeling all right Tommy?" she asked gently.

Tommy looked up and said. "Of course. Why?" he knew that it had come out too quickly. He looked away again and Martha put down her vegetable knife and sat down on the other side of the counter.

"Sweetheart, you know you can talk to me if you want to, please do."

Tommy could tell that she was trying very hard, but felt almost as uncomfortable in this situation as he did. He didn't feel any animosity towards her at the moment and maybe she could help him.

"I need to find out about the house," he blurted out, looking back at Martha, who raised her eyebrows in surprise.

"Oh? Why?" she was obviously relieved and

somewhat shocked. It was not what she had been expecting, she had expected him to be annoyed with his father and thought she would have to mediate between them. This may be an easier subject to discuss. She stood up again and picked up her knife and a bunch of baby carrots. "What would you like to know?"

"Everything."

Martha smiled. "Is that all?" They both smiled.

"I think you've been to the right place. When Clarissa and I first decided to move back into The Manor the villagers all warned me that there was something not quite right about the place. But I've not really had the opportunity to research it yet. Maybe that's a job for you and Clarissa over the Christmas holidays?"

Tommy visibly jumped at the prospect. Martha tried to change the subject.

"Why are you interested Tommy?" she put down her knife. "Is something worrying you?" Tommy quickly piled his vegetables into the waiting bowl.

"No. NO. Of course not," he knew this had come out too quickly, but he wasn't quite ready to share that much with Martha. He was still 'officially awkward' and desperate not to let her see him weaken.

"OK," she said flippantly, although she wondered to herself what had provoked this sudden interest. Thinking it for the best, she quickly changed the subject. "It's nice to see you getting along with Clarissa though, we were starting to worry about the two of you." Tommy shrugged and concentrated desperately on slicing his baby carrots to exactly the right thickness.

Suddenly a familiar voice interrupted. "What? You mean to say they haven't been fighting this morning?"

"Dad!" Yelled Tommy, forgetting the carrots and leaping to his feet. "What are you doing here?" Tommy's father had walked in whilst neither of them had been looking.

He feigned offence. "Oh well, if you're going to be like that, I may as well go back to work."

"Have you finished for today then?" asked Martha, almost sounding a little too relieved. Tommy's father leaned over the counter and gave Martha a peck on the cheek, and then he turned and picked Tommy up in a bear hug.

"I most certainly have. So, this afternoon when we have finished our lunch, I propose that we all go for a long walk around the lake. Then I'll buy us all a rather large ice-cream each." Tommy wriggled free and dashed off to tell Clarissa. Martha looked at Tommy's father.

"What's all this?" he enquired, pointing to the empty space Tommy had left at the breakfast bar.

"I have absolutely no idea," Martha replied truthfully. "But I'm not going to spoil it. Are you?" Tommy's father shook his head and moved around the kitchen to give her a proper hug.

Chapter 7

Presently the doorbell rang and Tommy went to answer it. He opened the door and there stood the small, scruffy but somehow distinguished form of Wilf. Wilf bowed, very low and then stepped forward extending his hand. He shook Tommy's hand quite hard and Tommy struggled not to yelp with pain.

Under his arm Wilf carried a large and awkward package of long and poorly rolled sheets of paper. They were so big that they had to be the maps from the library that was the only place Tommy had ever seen papers of that size.

Wilf came into the house and immediately the whole building seemed to take on a tranquil feeling. Tommy stopped and breathed deeply. Wilf put his hand on his shoulder.

"It is good," he said quietly. Tommy didn't understand, but he didn't want Wilf to know. Wilf had come to see him, not anyone else in the house, just him. Even though he wasn't expecting him, Tommy had somehow known that Wilf would turn up eventually.

"Would you like something to drink Wilf?" asked Tommy.

Wilf turned slowly and his beard waggled as he solemnly said. "Thank you, no. I have just eaten."

Tommy looked up at Wilf. His cardigan was still the threadbare and totally shapeless grey one he had worn last time Tommy had seen him.

"W... would you like to see my room?" Stammered

Tommy, not quite sure why Wilf had come to see him. The man nodded slowly, his eyes moving steadily around the whole of the entrance hall. He nodded now with more conviction and then softly he said.

"Even now the furnishing has changed it is almost as if I had never left."

Tommy's brow furrowed. "You used to live here?" he enquired and Wilf nodded slowly.

"That was a long time ago in your terms."

"My terms?" This did not reassure Tommy. Wilf moved toward the bottom of the staircase. He looked up them and smiled gently.

"This is a wonderful old house, don't you think?" Tommy nodded enthusiastically and led Wilf up the staircase. Wilf took his time, slowly making his way up the red carpet. He inspected every step and nodded his approval as he went, struggling slightly with the package under his arm. Tommy reached down and took the papers from him and they eventually made their way to the top step. Wilf breathed in deeply.

"I can still smell the mahogany panelling, Tommy. This takes me back at least four hundred years." Tommy had begun to be used to Wilf and smiled gently. He thought that this kind old man was obviously struggling with his senses and he thought that to be quite sad. Yet in other ways, he seemed so intelligent and alert. Tommy decided that he should learn all that he could from Wilf, before he lost all of his reasoning.

Suddenly Wilf stopped in his tracks. Tommy was startled and thought Wilf must be ill.

"Wilf, what is it?" he rushed to the old man's side and grabbed his elbow, as if to steady him. Wilf smiled passively down at him, his long beard waggled and he said quietly.

"My clock. You still have my clock in the exact same place." They both turned to look up at the face of the grandfather clock against the wall. Wilf stepped forward and Tommy struggled to hear what he whispered next.

"Hello old friend, I remember you. It has been many, many years since we last spoke." Wilf placed his left hand on the front panel of the clock and gently stroked the surface of the wood. To Tommy, it seemed as if a silence spread throughout the house. He could hear no sound from downstairs and there was, most unusually, no sound from Clarissa's bedroom. All that he could hear was the resounding thud from the clock's pendulum and the sound of his own heart beating. That was most unusual, he had only ever been conscious of his heartbeat whilst he lay in bed, yet he could hear and feel it quite clearly now.

Wilf remained by the clock and to Tommy it appeared that he was still speaking, but Tommy could not make out the words. Tommy noticed that his heart was now beating in time with the clock. What a coincidence. He stood transfixed by what he saw and to him it felt as if the ticking of the clock was slowing. He could feel his heartbeat slowing also and this scared him. He was not sure if he should speak, or for that matter whether he could speak. Wilf seemed to sense his fear and stepped away from the clock, putting his hand on Tommy's shoulder.

"Have no fear boy," he whispered. "There are many good and bad things in this world, but you have nothing to fear from me, or from this beautiful clock." Tommy opened and closed his mouth several times, but nothing seemed to want to come out. After what felt like an eternity, Wilf took the papers from Tommy and turned toward his bedroom. "Is this room the one in which you sleep?" Tommy suddenly sprang to life.

"Yes, please come in," he said, opening the door and flinging it wide. He became aware of the sounds around the house again, he could hear his father and Martha talking in the kitchen and he could hear faint strains of music from Clarissa's room. Wilf stood in the doorway and surveyed the room.

"Yes, this is a good choice," he stepped into the centre of the rug situated at the bottom of the bed and, strangely, the door closed slowly behind him and clicked shut. Tommy watched it in astonishment.

"Wilf," he began.

"Yes, dear boy. I am sure there are."

"Are what?" Tommy now considered that far from Wilf having a problem it was he who had lost his marbles. "What did I ask?"

"You were about to say that there are many things you do not yet understand and that you wish to ask questions of me." Tommy sat heavily on the end of the bed. Now, it seemed other people could hear his thoughts; this was just unbelievable.

"I... have to know why these things are happening to me," he said lamely. Wilf nodded and smiled. He waved the papers.

"That is why I have brought some of the most important maps I could find. We have to find the answer and we have to find it quite soon. There are moves and The Something is getting stronger." Tommy forgot to be scared and intimidated, now he was becoming annoyed.

"OK Mr Wilf, or whatever your real name is. I need to know things, firstly who are you? What is The Something? How will we find the answer and what will we do with it once we've found it?" Much to his irritation Wilf began to chuckle. "What's so funny?" Tommy really was starting to lose his temper now.

Wilf cleared a space on the floor, sat cross-legged in the middle of the rug and began to unroll the maps he had brought. Tommy instinctively sat next to him, he still wasn't happy but at least he might get a direct response now.

"Well young man," Wilf began "The funny part is that you ended your last question with a preposition. You do not pay heed to your studies, do you?" Tommy coloured slightly. Wilf went on. "No matter, no one is perfect. You asked: Who am I?" Tommy nodded eagerly. All the while Wilf was arranging the large maps around the floor. "I suppose the question really is: who 'was' I?" Tommy's face fell. This wasn't going to be easy. Wilf hurried on.

"You may not believe this, and that is your privilege. I am a druid, I have lived around here all my life and that is a very long time." Tommy puzzled over this for a few seconds.

"Aren't they extinct?" he asked. He had heard the name at school, but associated it with dinosaurs. Wilf began to laugh and his beard was twitching vigorously.

"Thomas, the dinosaurs were long since gone, when I came to be. I don't recall the exact year but it was somewhere around the Iron Age." Tommy grappled with this for a moment, and was beginning to think that Wilf was serious about this. How could that be? "I do not know quite how it is supposed to work, or if indeed it has happened as it should. I feel as though I have been preserved here for a purpose. The Something is a threat and I have to treat that as real." Tommy took a breath and interrupted.

"So what you're saying is," putting all the pieces together very quickly, he began to speak. All of his words tripped over each other. "You are a druid from hundreds of years ago, who lived in this house four hundred years ago, bought a grandfather clock that remembers you and you are here for a purpose." Tommy gasped for breath as he finished.

"That is quite a good summary, if a little confused and grammatically challenged." Tommy sat and studied Wilf carefully. He trusted this man, yet how could this be true? He had no time to ask, as the door swung open and in came Clarissa with a tray of home made lemonade and gingerbread men. Wilf and Tommy looked up, relieved at the interruption.

"So. Tommy," enquired Clarissa. "Is tracing the history of the house thirsty work?" Tommy nodded and stood up to take his lemonade. Clarissa put the tray on the dresser, moving Tommy's picture of his mother and father to one side. She glanced at Tommy as she did this and noticed his face.

"It's all right. I'll put them back when we've finished."

"I think we need to progress this, don't you?" Wilf smoothed the maps and Tommy responded.

"OK, would you like a gingerbread man?"

Clarissa looked at where Tommy was looking, but could see no one.

"What?" she asked. "Who are you talking to?" Tommy spun round.

"Wilf. Of course," he pointed to Wilf. "Wilf, this is Clarissa. Clarissa, this is Wilf." Wilf nodded slowly and returned his gaze to the plain, yellowed sheets. Tommy sat back down and poured over the other side of the map.

"Look," he said to Clarissa. "These maps show the area of the house many years ago. How far do they go back Wilf?" Clarissa began to edge toward the door.

"You've lost it, you know," she said, with one hand on the door handle. "You do know that there is nothing on the rug don't you? And, there's no one there, Tommy, you're talking to thin air. I'm going to tell Mummy," her voice had become thin and wavery, as if she were scared for some reason. Tommy shrugged and went back to the maps. He could hear Clarissa sprinting down the stairs.

"What exactly are we looking for?" he looked at Wilf for a while, contemplating why Clarissa had not admitted he was there. Wilf looked at him.

"You have absolutely no idea do you?" Tommy could feel himself going slightly red and he felt very small and foolish. He slowly shook his head and broke eye contact. "Then I shall tell you." Tommy sat enchanted whilst Wilf explained.

"I am," he began looking straight at Tommy. "A Druid. I am a good man," he added this in response to his change of face. "Many years ago, things were different and people lived by different values." Tommy nodded, he had learned about the Romans and the Tudors and they were all, if you asked him, quite brutal and totally mean to each other, but that was how it had been. Wilf continued. "I was the Arch Druid from this region and I worshipped on this ground," he looked very old and very tired at this point.

"This ground? This exact place?" Tommy was confused. "Why would you worship from a house?" Wilf shook his head slowly from side to side.

"A house has not always been here," Wilf said quietly. "This house most certainly has not, but there has been a dwelling here since after they moved the henge."

Tommy looked up. "Henge? Like Stonehenge?"

Wilf took off his glasses and rubbed his eyes. It was as if he despaired

"No. It was not like Stonehenge. It was before that. Stonehenge was started many years later. I was here long before that time. The notion was beyond Tommy's comprehension. Wilf nodded in reassurance. "Let me start at the beginning." Tommy stood up again, and went to the dresser to get some biscuits. As Wilf spoke, Tommy felt the same cool breeze he had felt several times before, brush past him. Picking up two gingerbread men, he went and sat back down, offering one to Wilf. Wilf took it and placed it gently on the edge of the top map.

"Many years ago…" Tommy could tell that Wilf was trying hard to be patient, even though there was not much time left. Tommy made a mental note that when Wilf had finished he must ask why they were in such a hurry.

"It is true. I was Arch Druid of Anglesea, the old name for this island you now call Great Britain. Do you know much about Druids Tommy?" Tommy nodded, munching gingerbread. "Tell me what you know then." Tommy swallowed half a mouthful without chewing and struggled to speak.

"A lot of them used to do magic and weird things to do with ghosts." Wilf sat open mouthed at this drivel and he became quite agitated.

"Where did you learn this?" he snapped. "Who taught you this nonsense?" Tommy moved away slightly, a little concerned at this outburst from Wilf.

"I, erm, I learned it at school. The history teacher told us, we did a project last year…" Wilf cut him short.

"It is no wonder the world is in such trouble," he wiggled his beard. "Would you like to hear my story?" Tommy nodded and relaxed a little.

"I shall continue." As he spoke, Wilf eyed the gingerbread man with more than a little apprehension. Tommy watched, but listened more intently. "Druidism is what I suppose you would say in this age, a religion. You have 'churches' do you not?" Tommy nodded. He understood this, so far. "In those churches, people congregate to pray to their God, Yes?" Another nod. "In my time we did not have churches, we had what are now called a 'henge'. A henge at my time was like Stonehenge in appearance. It was a circle of stones, built in a certain direction to catch the power of the Sun god and the Moon god at certain times of the day. This was when we would celebrate." Tommy was still following this but it was obviously going to be a long story, so he shuffled backwards and leaned against the end of the bed and tucked his knees up to his chin.

"Did you read the Bible?" Tommy thought this was quite a clever question, but Wilf chuckled.

"No. It was before the Bible existed."

Tommy tried to contemplate this and his brow furrowed. "What did you read then?"

"Later, we began to draw pictures to tell stories, but mostly we told each other things. Writing is only a recent invention in the history of everything." Now Tommy was starting to lose concentration. Wilf sensed this and went on with his tale. "Now, if you take your Bible as an example, it is a book that helps people to know what is right and what is wrong." Tommy understood this. He actually remembered that part of one of his lessons and he nodded consent to that. "If you imagine that your vicars and priests are people who explain the Bible to people and help them to be good, then I suppose Druids are something like that from a time before."

"This is like a science programme on the television," Tommy said eagerly. "I think I've seen a documentary programme that tells people about this sort of thing." Wilf sighed and Tommy fell silent again.

"Druids, or certainly this Arch Druid," he pointed at his chest "are good people in the main. Now to take your questions," Tommy had quite forgotten that he had asked any. "As you know this all happened a very long time ago before newspapers, radio or the television and many tales of the truth have been forgotten or sometimes embellished." Tommy could see the reasoning in that, but he was not one hundred per cent convinced and Wilf sensed this.

"Are you saying that you didn't do those weird things?" Wilf's eyes widened to Tommy's question.

"I most certainly did not. That is not in keeping with my belief, although I believe that some people did. It had nothing to do with the subject and teachings I had to give." Tommy smiled slightly, Wilf had gone slightly pink and Tommy wondered if he was not quite telling the whole truth.

"OK. You did have stone circles though." Wilf quickly regained his composure.

"I have already told that to you." Tommy nodded, suitably rebuked. "As for dancing around the henge at midnight, I'm afraid that did actually take place." Tommy was shocked. He had expected Wilf to deny that one. He hardly dared ask the next question.

"Did you dance around the henge?" Wilf's eyes lowered and it appeared to Tommy that he might cry. Slowly he began to nod.

"This is where all of this started." Tommy hadn't the slightest idea what 'all of this' was, but he didn't dare speak and let Wilf continue. "I will explain that in a moment. It is our belief that thieves, outlaws and offenders all deserve to be passed prematurely into their next life. We believe in re-incarnation."

"Re-incarceration?" enquired Tommy. Wilf chuckled.

"No dear boy. Do they not teach you anything these days? That is something entirely different. Re-incarnation is the belief that when someone dies, their soul continues to live in another body or form."

"Oh I see," agreed Tommy, wishing that he did.

"Quickly, your other questions and then we'll come back to the 'bad guys' as you would call them. Whenever you examine people, there are always some who will take advantage of others less fortunate. If you consider this along with vulnerable people who need someone to tell them what to do, you can get into all sorts of trouble."

"Trouble?"

"Oh yes. I was in a position of power and people believed everything I said to them. Now, some so-called Druids started proclaiming that they could hear and see things from the next lives of very bad people. Some of them began to tell people that they knew what was going to happen next and a whole new set of rogue Druids began to operate. Over time, the tales grew taller and I think we must all have been given the same reputation. There have been tales of good people being executed, of drunkenness and many other unimaginable things."

"Why haven't you explained to people that these things just aren't true?" Tommy couldn't understand that. If Wilf was here explaining to him, then why couldn't he explain to everyone else? Tommy picked up Wilf's gingerbread man. "Don't you want this? Martha does make good cakes." Wilf looked at it with suspicion.

"What is it?" he asked, taking it between his forefinger and thumb and sniffing gently.

"Try it," said Tommy. Wilf broke off a piece of leg and put it slowly into his mouth.

As he chewed, he began to smile and broke off another piece. "Strange really, that you think me to be unusual, yet you seem quite content to eat little people. That is something I have never done." Tommy grinned.

"Yes you have. You're doing it now." Wilf nodded in defeat. "Do you want to hear the rest of the story?" Tommy was struggling now with the weight of information that he was taking on board.

"Is there much more?" he asked and Wilf nodded.

"This is the most important piece and explains why you are involved."

"Involved? Involved in what? I'm not involved in anything, am I?" Tommy could feel his mouth going dry and he reached for his lemonade. His hand was shaking slightly as he raised the glass to his mouth. Wilf looked directly at him and his face became quite solemn.

"The main aim of my kind of Druid was to be at one with nature. If you like, we were ancient 'hippies'. I think that is the modern term." As Wilf spoke, Tommy couldn't help himself and grinned widely. His vision of a hippy was a skinny lad in massive flares, a luminous T-shirt and long scruffy hair similar to the photographs he had seen of his Dad in his younger days. Wilf was still speaking and Tommy tried to concentrate again. "If it was necessary to make an offering of a gift, it was done at the stroke of midnight. That is when the night is most dark and the Sun god cannot see. That is why midnight is still called 'the witching hour'." Tommy caught his breath, he had heard of that, but had no idea where the saying had come from. Suddenly he thought of the clock and last night's adventure. The clock that would not strike twelve and this was supposedly the same clock that Wilf had bought so many years before.

Things were definitely not what they seemed and Tommy could feel the hair on the back of his neck begin to stand on end. Wilf's story appeared to be gathering evidence and the more outrageous it became, the more convinced Tommy was to become. Wilf nodded again, as if to acknowledge that Tommy was beginning to come to terms with this tale.

"Over many years, the tales of speaking to people whose souls have departed this earth has become something of a tradition. It was celebrated on a date which these days is called November the first and this date used to be called 'All Souls Eve'."

"We have Halloween on October the thirty-first. That's the night before," Tommy said, gathering enthusiasm. Wilf dismissed this and continued.

"As my time as Arch Druid went on, I could tell that something was not what it seemed to be. As more people undertook evil deeds and thoughts, things began to happen. Slowly all of this bad energy manifested itself into an entity." Tommy was completely lost now. Was he still having the same conversation? He could not tell. Wilf hesitated and tried again.

"Every time someone bad died, it seemed as if all of their nasty negative thoughts and deeds were put together and turned into something real and unpleasant. Each one joined the previous one and the whole thing became something evil." Tommy's mouth fell open and the hairs on his legs, arms and the edges of his face all stood directly on end.

"The Something," he whispered, gingerbread crumbs rolling gently down the front of his sweatshirt. Wilf nodded.

"Yes," Wilf said quietly. "The Something. Although that is not all." Tommy did not want to hear any more and he stood up quickly. "Sit down Thomas." Wilf's voice had changed and was strong and commanding. "You must hear the rest of this tale." Tommy sat on the end of the bed with a thud.

"What rest?" he whispered as if someone, or

Something, might hear.

"After my time as Arch Druid it was not only 'bad feelings' that were sucked into The Something. Every war, every evil-doing donates all its negative energy into The Something. At first I could contain the thing with a mantra, or chant. Now in your time there are so many bad and evil things all over the world that I can no longer contain the force of the thing."

"What's that got to do with me?" Tommy was desperate to find a way out of this situation. "I haven't done anything wrong, have I?" Wilf shook his head.

"Oh no. That is not why I am here. You see. Arch Druids are very few and far between. They are born and not trained. You either are one or you are not."

"I'm definitely not," retorted Tommy putting the record straight. Wilf could certainly get that notion right out of his head.

"I think you are," replied Wilf and Tommy's heart sank.

"How do you know?" he was clutching at straws now.

"Arch Druids are always men folk. They have blond hair, blue eyes and their minds are open to 'other dimensions'."

"That's not me." Tommy backed toward the door.

"I think it is Tommy, and you know it to be true. If you consider your dreams, I would guess that you have dreams during the daytime. Also that since you have been in this house on the site of my henge you have had experience of all manner of thoughts and feelings." Tommy had lost this debate and he knew it to be so.

"Show me the henge on the maps then," Tommy demanded. "If you can." Wilf calmly smoothed the top map and showed Tommy where the house appeared. "Yeah. So?" Then Wilf slid out the bottom map, which was so old that Tommy could almost see right through it. This map was placed over the first and Tommy could see tree lines and roads that matched through from the map below. Slowly Wilf traced a circle on the map, which was pale and very hard to see. It fell right within the boundary of the outer walls. It was effectively inside the house on the lower map. Tommy could feel the sweat trickle down the middle of his back. What did this mean?

"Arch Druid Tommy," Wilf began in a very serious tone "I cannot contain The Something alone, I need your help. Will you help me Tommy?" As he asked this, he looked deep into Tommy's eyes and it felt as if he could see right inside his soul. Slowly Tommy began to nod his consent.

Chapter 8

A cool breeze lifted the edge of the top map as the temperature in the room dropped. Tommy froze, his eyes wide with fear, and he looked wildly about for evidence of an intruder. A shadow passed the window and both of them shot a glance at each other. Then the moment was passed and the sun shone again onto the rug on which they both sat.

"You see," Wilf said quietly. "You see why I need your help?" Tommy swallowed hard and nodded slightly, wondering where on earth all of this would end.

Wilf stood up and began to roll up his maps.

"I must go now," he said hastily. "This task must be complete before All Souls Eve."

"That's a week today, next Saturday," Tommy said breathlessly and Wilf nodded.

"Exactly, which is why we don't have much time." Wilf quickly walked to the door. "Is there anything you wish to ask me before I go?" he asked, turning with one hand on the door handle.

"Why couldn't Clarissa see you?"

"She is not an Arch Druid Tommy. You are."

"But what must I do?" Wilf opened the door and headed to the stairs, sliding his hand across the front of the clock as he did so. Tommy trotted after him. Suddenly it seemed that Wilf was desperate to leave and he was soon back at the front door. Tommy opened it and Wilf stepped out. "Again, what must I do?" Tommy was almost in a panic now, but Wilf looked over his half-rimmed glasses and said quietly.

"You will know when the time comes Tommy. You will know." With that he turned and walked quickly away down the drive.

"See Mummy, I told you he was acting funny." Suddenly Clarissa was standing behind him. "Tell Mummy who you were talking to then," she demanded.

"Wilf, of course." Tommy turned and closed the door.

"Who is Wilf dear?" enquired Martha, who appeared at the kitchen door, wiping her hands on a tea towel.

"He's the man from the library, I met him this morning. He came to show me the maps." Martha frowned.

"It's nice that you have friends dear, but you must let me know when you invite them here. Your father and I need to know who we are entertaining," she was not cross, but Tommy could tell that she was concerned.

"It's all right though," he continued. "He's gone for today. I might go and see him again." Martha nodded slowly and turned back into the kitchen.

David looked up as she walked in, and raised his eyebrows quizzically.

"I'm a bit worried," she started.

"Why?"

"Tommy seems to have developed an imaginary friend," David smirked.

"Don't laugh," Martha said sharply. "Has he had that sort of problem before?" David straightened his face.

"No. I don't recall ever having to deal with imaginary friends, although he does has a very fertile imagination." They both sat deep in thought for a while.

Clarissa followed Tommy back up the stairs.

"You better hadn't spoil the trip for Monday," she whispered hotly.

"Why? Where are we going?" Tommy asked absently, still concentrating mostly on what Wilf had said.

"Alton Towers," she said enthusiastically. "We have to be ready at six o'clock prompt, apparently."

"Why doesn't anyone tell me these things?" snapped Tommy, but Clarissa shrugged her shoulders and shot back into her bedroom.

Life can be difficult when you're an eleven-year-old boy who has persistent visions and everyone thinks you are a daydreamer. At eleven most boys have a vivid imagination, but usually that's associated with football heroes or they have a crush on the classroom glamour girl. Tommy had many reprimands at school and at home for retreating into his dream world. He took great satisfaction in being the only pupil to have this ability. However, what he didn't realise was that there was a purpose behind his recent dreams.

Saturday evening was rapidly approaching and the dinner Martha had prepared was his favourite. Dad must have mentioned it to her and she responded by presenting him with a huge plate of French fries and a hamburger the size of a mountain. The Saturday afternoon walk and ice cream had been deferred until another day. It was no great disappointment, after all there had been the promise of Alton Towers on Monday. Tommy managed to finish off with a bowl of fruit and ice cream. This was amongst sarcastic comments from Clarissa about dustbins and 'hollow legs'.

The last couple of days hadn't been too bad, he thought. Tommy had anticipated major arguments with Clarissa but much to his surprise, they had not happened. She had been an absolute pal for a mere girl. He thought – maybe, given time, he might even get to like her.

"May I be excused?" asked Clarissa. "I've finished

now."

"Me too," said Tommy.

"OK, but lights out at ten thirty. You can watch some television in Clarissa's room or play on her new computer."

"OK Dad." They both hopped off the dining chairs and disappeared upstairs.

"Well I never thought I'd ever see that, the two of them still actually enjoying each other's company. Miracles do happen, don't they David?"

"I'm not sure its a miracle, but there must be a reason for this. As I said before I'm sure its something to do with the house."

Tommy and Clarissa leapt up the stairs to Clarissa's bedroom. The sight of the grandfather clock caused Tommy to slow his pace and he kept it in full view, exercising caution as they passed it on the landing.

"Why did you do that Tommy? I've seen you do it before you've been daydreaming, especially when you climb the stairs." Clarissa had been very observant and was already suspecting that something was wrong. This and the sudden re appearance of Tommy from the library earlier in the day were both things that raised her suspicion. Tommy, however, did not want to involve her if at all possible. He was trying to deal with this by himself. He could just imagine the 'mega-hassle' he would get from his Dad if he landed Clarissa in any trouble.

"There's nothing wrong. It's just… it's just the clock. Yes, that's it. It's the clock."

"The clock?" As Clarissa turned, she faced the clock. "What's wrong with the clock? It's been in the family for ages. I know it's older than me."

"Oh, it's a little scary. Don't you think that it looks like it has eyes and frowns like Dad does a lot when I'm in trouble?" Clarissa stared hard at the clock face and the expression said it all.

"Yes, you're right. Look, it's packed its case and is going on a long holiday."

"Going on holiday?" Tommy was confused. "Packed its case? What do you mean? I don't understand."

"Tommy. It's called a long case clock. I was joking – it was a joke, didn't you get it?"

Flaming girls! They could be such a pain sometimes.

Tommy spun round on his heel and marched towards Clarissa's bedroom, turning back to her and saying.

"Well, are we going to play on your computer?"

"Of course," came the reply as she obediently followed him along the landing. Clarissa's room was tastefully decorated in exactly the colours one would expect a young girl's room to be. The usual favourite dolls and doll's house decorated its perimeter with twenty-first century technology scattered around in the centre. The equipment that took pride of place was a full thirty-six inch digital television with DVD and surround sound. In the opposite corner was a micro-stereo system that connected into the television and surround sound system with full FM/AM and CD player.

Next to her bed was a telephone in the shape of a banana and a mobile phone so small that even Tommy's smart eyes nearly missed its recognition. He entered the room then asked.

"Where is your computer?"

"Turn round dummy," Clarissa said flippantly. There it was, tucked behind the door. He stood fixed to the spot and his mouth sagged open. The equipment he had seen so far was impressive, but her computer was truly out of this world.

"Wow!" was his answer.

"I call you a dummy and all you can say is wow?"

"Wow!"

"Well at least you're consistent," muttered Clarissa.

"It's got a twenty-one inch flat screen, twin CD and DVD read-write drives – a floppy drive infrared keyboard and mouse." Tommy approached the computer still with his mouth open and inspected the apparatus more closely. "One hundred giga-byte hard drive and tape stream back-up, Pentium four chip operating at two giga-hertz with a giga-byte of RAM?" he questioned.

"You obviously know your computers, but how well do you operate them?"

"Just watch me." Tommy flipped a few switches and the computer responded instantly. Seconds later he had listed the various programmes on the hard drive and was selecting the best game to play.

"This key board is ace, absolutely ace." His fingers danced across the keyboard and the screen rapidly changed to operate the latest game release on the market.

"You've even got 'Underworld' on this. It only came out last week. Have you played it yet?"

"Not yet. I asked Mummy if we could have it because I knew you were stopping over this week. It was a surprise especially for you. I wasn't sure what kind of geek you would turn out to be, but I think I've got you sorted now." Tommy stuck his tongue out at her, but turned back to the screen

"Gee thanks! It's brill!" For the next couple of hours they both became enthralled by the game. They were absorbed by it's intricate programming and challenging skill levels. There was no doubt in Clarissa's mind: whatever their differences had been in the past she had seen a different side of Tommy this weekend.

Their yelps of delight and laughter echoed past the

grandfather clock and down the staircase and into the drawing room where David and Martha sat.

"Just listen to those two now. I can't believe the transformation. It's as if someone has cast a spell on them weaving them together. I expected the same old attitude from both of them this week. Tommy completely absorbed in his own little world and Clarissa stomping around complaining that she would rather have Tiffany here to stay than Tommy."

"Yes, the difference is remarkable," replied Martha. "It must be down to the fairy dust."

"Fairy dust? What's that?" David pulled a face. Was Martha making fun of him?

"Oh surely I've told you before about the fairy dust? I must have done."

"No you haven't. Tell me more, even though it sounds as if you're taking the Mickey. Foolish as I am I'll listen to what you have to say – Babe!" David kissed her on the cheek as Martha began to explain.

"Well the fairy dust goes back ages. I recall my grandmother telling me a tale of a fairy that came to visit her many years ago."

"Oh and I suppose the fairy's name was Tinkerbell and Peter Pan came to her rescue?" he scoffed.

"Now stop it, otherwise I won't tell you the rest of the story! It was my favourite bedtime story of all time. I would ask Nana time and time again to tell me. I never became tired of this one." The grandfather clock began to strike the hour. Its resounding chime echoed throughout the house as it struck ten o'clock.

"Actually the fairy's name was Twinkle. She was really quite a peculiar fairy in my opinion, she wore a pink tutu of all things. My grandmother's room was where Tommy is sleeping. And one night at around midnight on

Halloween I think, she had just finished reading Peter Pan. She was fascinated by the book and especially Tinkerbell and had talked of nothing else all week. She suddenly awoke at midnight and it just happened to be the thirty-first of October, although she swore that what happened next was not the result of daydreaming or sleep deprivation. Out of the blue appeared a bright light as big as a tennis ball and it darted all over the bedroom as if looking for something.

"At first it was so erratic that Nana thought it was moonlight playing tricks on her. She soon realised how real it was. Twinkle rested on the bottom of the bed, crossed her left leg over her right and smiled inquisitively at her. I think she was so shocked that words eluded her. In fact Twinkle broke the ice by introducing herself.

"'Hello. My name is Twinkle, what's yours?' Nana managed to find some words to give an audible reply by introducing herself and after a short time the two became quite friendly. She discovered that Twinkle was from a different world than ours, or at least a different place. For many years afterwards she searched for that place but she was never to find Twinkle again, nor did she want to discuss it with anyone.

"The fairy stayed with her all night and apparently they became very close friends. Twinkle explained that the world she came from was not like Nana's world, but a place you would associate with our 'Iron Age' period. Life was simple for the few people who lived there, but the increasing dangers that threatened the world appeared to be very real.

"As the night went on, gradually Twinkle's glow began to fade until eventually she disappeared and as I said was never seen again. How real it was when Nana told the story to her mother, it was subject to great debate as the tale was retold down through the generations."

Martha then stood up from her armchair and moved across to the china cabinet in the corner of the room. The door swung open and she reached for a small pillbox, whereupon she removed the lid and revealed a very fine glittering dust.

David stared inside the box and his eyes widened at the sight of the dust. A glow seemed to radiate from the contents, a glow that was perceived by him to be full of goodness and seemed to draw him closer. He was barely inches away, still fascinated by the sight of the glow, which was reflected quite clearly in his eyes. It was a truly amazing event. He had never seen anything quite like it and his attention was totally focused upon the pillbox.

"David... David... DAVID! Are you all right?" Martha pushed him away and quickly replaced the lid on the pillbox. Within seconds David shook his head and regained his composure.

"What in heaven's name was that? I've never experienced anything like that before. It's fascinating."

"You're right there, but that's the story and power of fairy dust. You will have to make up your own mind about Nana's tale. I'm surprised I've never mentioned it before. It was such a large part of my childhood."

"No, indeed, it was quite a tale. At first, I thought it was just a childhood imagination, much like Tommy's... but now I've seen the dust. It puts a completely different angle on the story."

"The dust was collected off Nana's bed the next morning. Her mother put it into that pillbox, which has been in the family since that day. Yes, it's truly an odd tale and the dust seems to give it some positive credibility if you believe that kind of thing."

They both chatted for a short time and decided to

retire early. The clock had struck eleven. Everyone in the house had heard the chime.

"You two pack up your stuff now and get into bed," Martha instructed. David repeated the instructions and added the word, "Quickly." Their bedroom door closed and Tommy and Clarissa continued to play quietly on the computer.

"Did you hear Mummy? She wants us to pack up and go to sleep. It is getting late." Tommy briefly ignored her, deeply engrossed in the game he was playing.

"Just a few minutes more," he pleaded. "I'm just moving to level eight. There are only two more levels to go." Clarissa was becoming a little bored. Tommy had taken over the computer and her interest in the game had disappeared over an hour ago. As time approached midnight, Clarissa went and changed into her pyjamas. They were quite fashionable as sleep wear goes, but Tommy had not even noticed, he was totally engrossed in the game and totally committed to finishing level ten.

"There," he proudly announced. "The highest skill level. That was superb. Thanks Clarissa for the game, I really enjoyed that. Once you manage the first three or four levels the rest is just a matter of time and concentration," she yawned through both lack of sleep but moreover through boredom. Although Clarissa had enjoyed the last two days, it was getting late.

"Good," she replied. "Are you going to your room now? Don't make a noise and wake Mummy and David. Otherwise we're both in deep trouble."

"OK," said Tommy, still fresh and not at all sleepy. He crept gingerly across the landing. As he started his journey the grandfather clock began to strike midnight. Six, seven, Tommy counted to himself and wished that the floorboards did not creak quite so loudly. Clarissa would never forgive him if he woke the rest of the house. Eight, nine, he was a metre away from the clock. Ten, eleven, oh how he cursed these floorboards.

He reached his bedroom and suddenly realised that the clock had not struck twelve. Yet the fingers on the face both pointed to twelve. Apparently this clock would only strike at each thirty-minute interval. Tommy thought that clocks struck every quarter of the hour. Slowly it dawned on him that the ticking, or should he say 'tocking' had stopped.

Tommy turned and stared at the clock face. In the semi-darkness he was convinced the clock had a personality of it's own. Although very plain in design, it was quite oppressive and intimidating and he found himself hurrying past and toward his bedroom door. As he turned the handle on the bedroom door, it clicked and released the door from its frame. Tommy passed through and closed it dutifully behind him. The clock still filled his mind and for some reason he stood and contemplated his situation. He was not uncomfortable but his mind was not yet ready to rest. There was something else, something that kept him from his bed and he couldn't quite work out what it was, yet there was definitely 'something' in his room. He clutched at the bed-cover, ready to snatch it over his head. What possible use would that be if there were someone in the room with him? The duvet and bedspread would be no use whatsoever as protection against attack.

"Hello?" he enquired. "Clarissa, is that you?"

"I shouldn't wait if I was you, you'll be here all night before it strikes twelve." Tommy had to agree with that. It was definitely a very long pause.

Hold on. Who had said that? Had he gone to sleep? No, he thought not. His heart hammered in his chest it was not a familiar voice.

"Who's there?" he cried.

"No. Oh no, no, no, no, no, no. It's a mini human being. You are not supposed to be in this room." It was shrill and quite high-pitched and possibly a little rough in tone.

"Hello?" he whispered, still clutching the quilt to his face. "Is someone there?" he held his breath and listened to the silence. The silence suddenly became very, very loud. Eventually, as he waited it began to pound in his ears. He began to think he had imagined the voice, when something gently began to tug at the edge of the quilt to his left. He'd definitely heard or rather felt something then. Tommy had not been able to turn on the light and the sounds were coming from the direction of the fireplace, although there was no one there.

"Down here. That's right, this way." The voice had become softer, but still retained the qualities as before. Tommy's eyes became very wide and the effort to move his head became great. He barely dared to breathe in again, in case the sound covered something he should hear.

He became somewhat nervous and fearful of what would happen next. Darkness did not normally frighten him. As he looked down toward his left, he became aware of a shape. A shadowy figure had begun to materialise between him and the fireplace. It was an outline so mysterious yet without fear or threatening. It was reminiscent of a small hunchback, child-sized person, yet somehow the shape had the feeling of great age. Tommy tried to focus on the figure and decided definitely not to turn on the light. It was true. There was someone or something in his room. How many times had he thought or dreamed of this, only to be reassured that it was his imagination playing tricks on him? Yet this time, the thought appeared to be real. This person, however small, began to tug in earnest at the side of the quilt.

The outline began to take shape in the dim moonlight that shone through the window. The creature stood approximately a metre in height (although according to Tommy that was thirty-nine inches in real measurement – he had never really converted to metric measurement).

"Tommy, look at me. I'm not that distasteful that you can't bare to look at me, surely?" Tommy didn't know what to do. His mouth opened and closed several times, yet no sound came. At first he thought he should call for his father, and then slowly as the small person seemed to present no physical threat, he attempted to ask something. Yet still no words came out of his mouth.

A small, knurled old face looked earnestly up at him and the creature's eyes flashed with a childish devilment. His facial features had been first to materialise and could only be described as 'goblin-like' in appearance. The nose was covered in lumps and bumps and warts and was so long that it could have been used as a fishing pole. His ears were big and pointy, their shape had features of purpose and that was of the most sensitive hearing ever. His eyes looked like goldfish bowls, big and stark, capturing all around him, yet friendly to those who accepted him.

"Thomas Ravensdale." A sharp utterance seemed to bring him back to where he was. "Will you speak?"

A funny shaped hat dominated his cranial features and the red and white stripes reminded Tommy of a football supporter. The creature in front of him had now fully materialised, its face became stern and Tommy knew he would have to force himself to say something and he tried really hard.

"I… Erm, you are…? What are you doing? Erm…"

then he gained a little confidence. "I'm Tommy. My name is Tommy, what's yours?" This amused the creature.

"Well at least I've had the courtesy to introduce myself, which is more than can be said for some people…" Tommy snatched the quilt back indignantly and the small person laughed. It was quite a friendly laugh and it wasn't at all threatening.

"You're quite right little man. My name is Hoy-Paloy! You are a townie and not an urbanite. Would 'ave to be a townie. Why do I get all the 'orrible jobs? I suppose it will 'ave to do." With this, the small person let go of the quilt and stooped in a serious and most formal bow, so deep that his beard lay almost flat on the wooden floorboards. Hoy-Paloy stretched out his arm as a gesture, revealing a hand of strange proportions. His fingers were long and wiry, almost skeleton-like with nails that extended almost an inch from his finger-ends.

Tommy shook Hoy-Paloy's hand, but to his surprise the touch felt strange though somehow reassuring. The moonlight streamed in through the window and touched both of them, casting a shadow across the bed. The strangeness was that there was only the shadow of one little boy with an outstretched arm.

The creature's clothes were just as bizarre and colourful as the rest of the character in front of him. The shoes most definitely had to be the most outstanding feature of this creature. They were big and awkward. Tommy thought to himself 'How on earth does he manage to walk in those shoes?'

"What's a 'Hoy-Paloy'?" thought Tommy. 'Where on earth had that come from?' Tommy had no idea. The creature stopped abruptly.

"I'm a 'who', not a 'what'," he snapped. Tommy could tell by his tone that this indeed mortally offended him and he tried to make amends.

"I'm most terribly sorry, Hoy-Paloy. Please forgive my ignorance. I'm not used to talking to unannounced people in the middle of the night. I must have been still a little drowsy." That seemed to work and Hoy-Paloy stood slightly awkwardly to the side of the bed and waited. He stood there on the same spot with his eyes fixed on the figure in front of him. He strained his vision to focus more to determine what, or quite rightly who was in front of him. To Tommy it seemed like an eternity, what on earth was he supposed to say next? As they looked at each other, Tommy could see the twinkle in Hoy-Paloy's eyes and the very small trace of a smile around the edges of his mouth and slowly he began to relax. Eventually he broke the silence that had developed.

"What?"

"What? What?" came the response.

"You're laughing."

"Am I?" his beard began to twitch most suspiciously.

"Yes," Tommy was becoming exasperated "you know you are, don't fib."

"I don't fib. I'm here to take you to solve the question."

Tommy stopped.

"What question?"

"You know the question." Hoy-Paloy suddenly became very serious.

"Do I?" Tommy felt most uncomfortable again.

"Yes. You have felt The Something and you know it is on the move. I am here to help you and we must stop it between us."

Tommy could feel so many questions welling up inside him. His thoughts flashed back to Wilf. Wilf had talked about 'The Something' as if it had been an entity.

How could Hoy-Paloy know about The Something? More to the point, why was he even contemplating these things? He was not involved. If these strange folk had a problem what had it got to do with him, Tommy, the chap who always got into trouble for daydreaming?

"Oh, but Tommy, it's got everything to do with you. You are the only one that can save us." Tommy visibly jumped.

"What?" Hoy-Paloy couldn't have heard that surely? After all, he was only thinking it and hadn't said anything had he? He collected his composure. "Save whom, and from what?" There was another pause. Hoy-Paloy studied him closely and then extended an old and knurled hand toward him.

Additional lighting was definitely needed in the room and Tommy reached out for the light switch. He flicked the switch and instantly the character in front of him danced in a dizzy rage, mumbling and grumbling about 'townies'. His dancing was not in the least artistic it could only be described as funny and amusing. Tommy roared with laughter at the sight of this strange person stomping all over the carpet and uttering in a language although indecipherable strangely resembling obscene curses.

"Turn off the light," Hoy-Paloy pleaded. "Turn it off, turn it off."

Tommy responded instantly realising that this action had clearly infuriated the little being.

'Click' the electric light responded to the switch and within seconds the moon replaced the light within the bedroom. Again the strange creature stood in front of him and there was no ranting or raving as of a few seconds before.

"That was a very stupid thing to do. Goblins don't like bright lights. Don't do it again." Hoy-Paloy barked.

Tommy's response was instant.

"Yes Sir." Tommy was not quite sure whether the character in the bedroom was fictitious or not, but it seemed like a good idea to agree with him.

"Now sit on the bed and I'll explain to you why I'm here." Not only was the sight of the goblin funny in appearance but his high shrill voice fitted perfectly to his character.

"This is extremely important. The future of the Kingdom depends on you. I have been sent to lead you through the gateway and into The Kingdom." Tommy sat in awe, still mystified by the mere presence of this character in his bedroom. The words Hoy-Paloy had already spoken had not registered with Tommy. Therefore he could not recollect their meaning.

"Are you listening to me boy? This is important. Don't you understand? The Kingdom depends on you. Our entire existence is in the balance. The forces of evil are becoming dominant and only the 'one' can save what now remains of the Kingdom."

"Erm, pardon? Erm, I'm only eleven years old. What do you mean Kingdom? The 'one'?" Tommy was beginning to improve his listening skills, although it was looking difficult to also improve his reassuring skills.

"I am not one for explaining things properly, but I'm very well intentioned. Sometimes things go wrong. It could be my fault, but that's because other people have not explained it properly."

'All very confusing.' Tommy thought 'but it's really fun having a goblin in my bedroom, whether I'm dreaming or not.' Still the words from this creature made no sense.

"Where do you come from? Why are you here? What are you? How did you get into my room? What did you mean by the 'one'? Where is The Kingdom?"

"Stop. Stop, stop. Too many questions. I have to answer one at a time otherwise I get confused. Now ask me again slowly this time and let me think of the answer."

"Where do you come from?"

"Right. That's easy," muttered Hoy-Paloy. "I come from the Kingdom and before you ask where that is, at least I can remember that was another question, it's far away."

"What do you mean, far away? How far?"

"That's too difficult and Fliw the Hermit will have to answer that when we get there. He knows everything."

"Why are you here Hoy-Paloy?"

"That's easy. I've been sent from the Kingdom to bring you back. You're our only chance of survival, in fact the only chance of both worlds' survivals. Both worlds are threatened with extinction and you are the only one who can save us."

"Me? Extinction? The one? Hoy-Paloy, your answers are creating more questions. I'm puzzled by your answers."

"Don't be. Fliw will explain it all far better than I can after I have delivered you."

"Hoy-Paloy, what are you?"

"I'm a goblin from The Kingdom. My claim to fame is that I was once very friendly with a certain wizard of a very important round table King. My job is the gatekeeper to this world and The Kingdom. See, this is the key from my world into yours." Hoy-Paloy held up a golden key some six inches in length and it glistened in the moonlight. The locking end looked quite intricate, suggesting the door it opened must be very important. A golden chain wrapped itself around his neck and through the key, securing it firmly to the gatekeeper.

"This is the return key from your world to mine." This

key, as Hoy-Paloy held it into the moonlight, was a much smaller key, only about one inch long, and again secured to the gatekeeper by a golden chain.

"So where exactly is the door then?" Tommy asked.

"The door is there behind you," he pointed to Tommy's bedroom door.

"The bedroom door?"

"No, No, No, the door behind the grandfather clock is the way to The Kingdom and the door behind the fireplace is the door from The Kingdom."

"Behind the clock? There is no door behind the clock. It has a solid front." Tommy was confused.

"Exactly. The door is 'behind' the clock."

"I see," said Tommy, wishing that he did. "And the keys activate the doors."

"Well, not quite. It's the key and the gatekeeper, that's me by the way, that activate the doors."

"Ah," Tommy nodded in agreement. "But the grandfather clock only struck eleven and then it stopped."

"Yes, that's right. I usually travel at midnight between the two worlds, the clock never strikes twelve, otherwise I couldn't be here. It will start again once I leave this side."

All of these events were difficult to grasp for an eleven-year-old boy, but Tommy thought it was part of his daydreaming and was happy to go on with the conversation. He had no fear, which in his situation was to prove quite valuable in the voyage he was about to undertake.

"Is there anything else you should tell me Hoy-Paloy? Have you forgotten anything?"

"No. No, no, that is all. Now hurry, we must go. There is no time to waste." Tommy hesitated knowing he must tell his Dad if he went anywhere. He thought if it was only a dream then the adventure he was about to undertake would also be a dream and therefore he didn't have to ask if he could go with Hoy-Paloy. This was a real dilemma for Tommy and he stood contemplating the possible outcomes and solutions to this puzzle. He had to solve it, yet somehow he knew he was to do it alone. The look on his face clearly indicated his father's rules of knowing where he was all the time.

"Hoy-Paloy, I'm going to tell my Dad where we're going."

"Can't do. Won't do. Can't do. Fliw the Hermit says so. Must be something to do with the balance of the worlds and the universe or so he tells me. It isn't safe to tell anyone. It's our secret." Tommy again gave consideration to Hoy-Paloy's words. Anyhow, it was only a dream wasn't it? He thought. I may as well enjoy the adventure because I will wake up in the morning in this bed safe and sound.

"Let's go Hoy-Paloy and save The Kingdom!" Hoy-Paloy guided Tommy to the door of the bedroom and opened it quietly; outside, the landing was quiet and still. Slowly they crept out onto the threadbare carpet leading to the stairs, Hoy-Paloy leading and Tommy following with a small knot of apprehension sitting deep in the pit of his stomach.

The only sound to be heard in the absolute darkness was the resounding tock, tock, tock of the clock. They stood quietly looking up at the face and the face, plain and cold as it was, appeared to smile passively back at them and somehow it was still visible in the pitch dark. After what seemed like an eternity, Tommy was just about to suggest that they went back into his room, when Hoy-Paloy turned to him and took a deep breath. Suddenly he burst into a rhyme and Tommy gazed in amazement. Surely his father must be able to hear this?

"Hoy-Paloy is on his way.

He has a task to do this day.

Fliw the mystic made me this charm.

The purpose of which is to keep us from harm.

Pretty flowers and forests too.

Can we save them? Tommy, it's up to you."

Tommy instinctively drew back, but Hoy-Paloy pulled him forward and he felt compelled to go with the little creature. As they passed toward the door the creature turned to him.

"We're only safe as long as the clock is ticking in this world. The clock always ticks. If it stops then we have lost all hope." Tommy's eyes widened.

"What do you mean?" he resisted and pulled his hand away.

"Oh don't worry." Hoy-Paloy flapped his hands in dismissal. "I wind the clock every twelve hours without fail. I've never let it stop and it's ticked quite happily for at least three hundred and fifty years to my recollection." Tommy stood with his mouth wide open and waited for something sensible to come to mind. After a few moments it hadn't. Hoy-Paloy reached for his hand and pulled him further toward the clock.

Tommy stepped forward and closed his eyes.

"Now follow me Tommy, and be careful. Do exactly as I say." Hoy-Paloy removed the small gold key from around his neck and inserted it into a lock. Tommy had never noticed this keyhole at the side of the front casing of the clock. What was strange though was that there was no apparent door to open. He turned the key clockwise and suddenly a vision of a door appeared; it was the same door that he had seen in his dreams on previous occasions. This was the most peculiar house Tommy had ever stayed in and he wasn't sure he could take in all this abstract information.

As the key was turned, the door began to open. Tommy studied this carefully, doors usually opened in the opposite direction. He had no time to contemplate further as he observed the sight appearing before him. He felt the sensation that he was again in his dream world; no floor, no ceiling, yet this time he had a companion with him. This time there were no strange lights at the end of the tunnel. The journey with Hoy-Paloy seemed to have purpose.

"This way. This way," ordered Hoy-Paloy. "Remember, do exactly as I say and now hold my hand," he reached for the door, the mechanism clicked and the door swung wide open to reveal a strange, but dimly lit room.

"I've dreamt about that door. So where are we now?"

They entered the room and the door behind them slammed shut and disappeared.

"Welcome to my home," Hoy-Paloy announced. "Now, firstly the keys must be placed in the golden casket for safety. Only the gatekeeper can open the casket." Sure enough, over on the far side of the room lay a beautifully engraved casket in which Hoy-Paloy placed the two golden keys. As he walked away, to Tommy's complete amazement the casket disappeared. 'Wow, now that's impressive security,' he thought to himself.

Tommy's eyes began to focus on his surroundings.

"This looks like a home."

"It sure is. Ain't it something? It has all the modern conveniences, look, running water," (which turned out to be a mountain stream running through the cave). "Light," he pointed upwards to where a hole in the roof allowed moonlight to stream through to light the cave softly. "Constant hot water and an oven for cooking." There was a bubbling geezer and red-hot hole in the rock that must have been heated by some volcanic action. Except for a few comforts like a wooden chair, a blanket and pots and pans in a wooden cupboard his home looked positively prehistoric.

"I suppose goblins live like this?" Tommy enquired.

"Oh no. I'm very privileged, living in this comfort. Other goblins are not as fortunate." Tommy decided to abandon this line of conversation and investigate his surroundings.

"What's outside your cave?"

"My cave? My cave, my cave. It's not a cave," ranted Hoy-Paloy. "It is my home, my habitat. It is not a mere hole in the rock."

"Sorry. I didn't mean to offend you. Can you show me the outside of your home please?"

"Follow me. I'll take you to Fliw the Hermit. He will explain all of this to you and the quest you are here to undertake." Tommy followed Hoy-Paloy out of his home. Dawn was just breaking and the sight before him was, in natural terms, just breathtaking. A lush countryside surrounded them flocks of birds swirled in the sky and animals were in abundance around them. A vixen and her cubs casually strolled past completely oblivious of Tommy and Hoy-Paloy and seemingly without a care in the world.

A trail from Hoy-Paloy's home wound down the hillside and disappeared into the vast woodland beyond and ran over the horizon. A bright yellow sun crept over the horizon and cast it's warmth across the countryside. Then mouth ajar, Tommy pointed to the sky: there was a second sun, right next to the first.

"The Kingdom has two suns?"

"Why yes. It also has three moons. Is that strange?"

"This is unbelievable. These sights are nothing at all like those at home. Where are the roads and the cities?"

"The roads and the cities? We have none of those. There is no need. The life we lead here does not require them." Hoy-Paloy again broke out into rhyme with almost a skip in his stride. The seriousness of his mission had disappeared as they made their way through the dense undergrowth.

Tommy gazed back over the trail they had followed so far, it led to a hole in the hill that Hoy-Paloy had called home. The shadows followed Hoy-Paloy along the trail created by the two suns, yet Tommy had no such shadow in his wake.

"Fliw's house lies at the end of this trail by the lake, just a few more minutes and we'll be there." Sure enough there stood a cabin, with a lake behind it. A trickle of smoke floated gently from the brick chimney. Hoy-Paloy knocked at the ill-fitting door, which rattled on its hinges as it swung open.

"Fliw. Fliw, are you there? I've delivered 'the one' as you asked." Out of the dark emerged a figure, head bent and supported by a wooden staff. His clothes resembled sackcloth similar to a medieval monk and a mass of grey spiky hair draped down over his collar. The figure stood about one metre away from Tommy and slowly Fliw lifted his head.

"Wilf. Wilf, is that you? It's Tommy, don't you remember me?" The person stood before him was the exact image of Wilf from the library. What on earth he was doing here Tommy could not begin to think. 'I must still be in my dream' he contemplated, 'I must be imagining him.' This solution seemed more than plausible to Tommy and he accepted the person in front of him as Wilf's twin.

"My name is Fliw the Hermit. Please sit down Tommy. I hope that this is not too frightening for you?"

"But it's my dream," Tommy replied. "I'm not frightened because I can't be hurt in my dreams. It's not real."

"If you say so Tommy. Please allow me to explain why I asked Hoy-Paloy to seek you out and bring you to me." Fliw studied Tommy from his blond hair and blue eyes down to the white trainers he wore on his feet. This was 'the one', the answer to the crisis that faced the Kingdom. "Now Tommy again please don't be frightened and when I explain the following to you please keep an open mind. I know it all feels so unreal but you are here to serve a purpose.

"When the universe was created, planets existed in two dimensions. One is where you are now and the other is where you came from. The equilibrium between the two dimensions is finely balanced. So critical is this balance that, for instance, as Hoy-Paloy moves between worlds, time stops until that balance is restored. There is also a balance between good and evil between worlds where both worlds have an equal amount of both. Any significant shift of either between worlds would be disastrous for that world. In other words, if evil from this world crossed over to your world then the results would be catastrophic.

"To ensure this balance exists for all time, many mystics, or druids, as you would know them have been entrusted with the secret of the doorway. The gatekeeper holds the keys to the doorways. You've already met him. He's called Hoy-Paloy the goblin." Fliw turned his head. "How old are you Hoy-Paloy?"

"I will be one thousand five hundred and thirty next birthday. However, I lost count for a while last century. So I may be younger than that really!" answered Hoy-Paloy.

"The gatekeeper has a great responsibility thrust upon him by the mystics who protect both him and the doorways from all things evil. You may have learned from your history books of wizards such as the great Merlin, of druids and alchemists. These have, through your world, kept the secrets and held it with the mystics of this world. During the last two hundred years in your time, as your world has developed, people have believed less and less in magical powers and your mystics have become almost extinct. As your mystics lose their powers and die, ours must suffer the same leaving the evil powers within this world with an increased strength. This strength has begun to threaten both of our worlds.

"If our evil can manage to cross the boundary to your world, all life as we know it would cease to be. It would be Armageddon for both worlds. My powers are weak and no longer strong enough to protect the doorway. As the days go by in my world I can feel the evil growing stronger and my ability growing ever weaker. Tommy, we have brought you through the gate to reinforce my powers. Although your age is somewhat young, you are the one who shall save us all from The Something."

"What do you think The Something is Fliw? Hoy-Paloy mentioned it and so did Wilf in my world."

"Yes, so far you have been lucky. The characters you are about to meet are 'the good guys' as you would put it in so many words. The Something is an entity that can appear differently to anyone, it reflects individual fears and weaknesses. Throughout time, all the evil that has been created in your world and mine has accumulated into this 'Something'. Our two worlds are quite different, a fact of which I am sure you have already discovered.

"This evil grows stronger as time passes, even more so over the last one hundred years where the wars in your world have accelerated this threat to both our civilisations. The mystics have kept this force in place over time through the gatekeeper. As I have said though, my powers are weakening and a new counter force is needed to restrain The Something."

"But I'm only eleven years old. What do you expect me to do? I don't think my Dad will approve."

"Oh don't worry, you have hidden powers that you are not aware of and it is my mission to help you to develop them, to protect the gatekeeper and to restrain The Something."

"Oh," said Tommy, who thought for a few seconds and then responded, "Well, Daddy always says I should help people, especially old people." Fliw threw him a glance; if only he knew exactly how old he was. "OK, what do you want me to do? When do I get to meet The Something?"

"Oh there's plenty of time for that. I want you to meet some of my friends too, but first of all I think you should return through the gate. Then I think you should come back tomorrow and begin your training. Time in this world does not pass in the same way as it does in yours. Before you get used to it, the most important thing is for you to develop your power. Hoy-Paloy?"

"Yes Fliw?"

"Please take Tommy back through the gate, I think he has had enough for today. After all, he is only eleven years old." Fliw smiled at Tommy as he said this and he ushered them both to the door. "I will see you on the morrow. Hoy-Paloy will fetch you and escort you through the gate again."

"But Fliw, there is so much that I need to ask you. There are so many questions to be answered and when will I have the chance?"

"Don't worry about that. The important things are your powers and whilst they are developed, to keep The Something away until both of us are strong enough to do battle with this evil."

"It still sounds beyond the capability of an eleven year old. Anyhow, what powers do I have? Are they like Superman's?"

"No. No, don't go jumping off a cliff because you may get a nasty shock. All I will say before I bid you farewell for now, is that your powers will become vast. So strong in fact that..." Fliw stopped himself, waved Tommy goodbye and closed the door.

"Let's go Tommy. I need to get you back to the gateway as quickly as possible, there are dangers lurking in the woods that both of us don't want to face."

He nodded in agreement and quickly followed Hoy-Paloy back through the undergrowth. As they approached the doorway to Hoy-Paloy's cave Tommy became aware of the quietness around him and Hoy-Paloy's pace doubled almost to a sprint. The sky darkened and threatened with a sudden menacing storm and beyond the quietness a cackle echoed more frightening than the sky above them.

"What was that Hoy-Paloy?"

"No time to talk, quickly into my home." They both disappeared through the heavy oak door and it closed with a thud behind them. Hoy-Paloy breathed a sigh of relief and pointed toward his open fireplace.

"Go on, through the fireplace and you'll be back in your bedroom. Go quickly, please," he gasped. Realising that Hoy-Paloy wasn't joking, Tommy moved to the fireplace, Hoy-Paloy turned the golden key and Tommy disappeared only to find himself immediately returned to his bedroom. He felt bewildered about his adventure and wondered if anyone would believe what had happened. He knew his Dad would 'pooh-pooh' it, blaming it on his active imagination.

'I wonder if Clarissa would believe me?' he pondered. 'I must tell someone.'

He hopped into bed realising that he must by now be tired, but he became aware that the grandfather clock on the landing was ticking again. He wondered exactly how long he had been away; it felt like hours. Curiosity eventually got the better of him and he tiptoed out onto the landing. The clock showed one minute past midnight. Only a minute, he'd only been away for one minute. This was by far the weirdest dream he had ever had. Struggling with the 'time' issue he crept back to bed and was soon fast asleep.

Chapter 9

Tommy woke early on the Sunday morning, most perturbed by his experience the previous night. At that point however he was convinced it had all been some sort of really wild dream and he had to admit he was prone to a little dreaming. He got up and opened the bedroom door. The house was quite quiet and no one was about. He tiptoed carefully along the carpet to the grandfather clock. He looked up at the great timepiece and it stared coldly back at him. What had he expected, that it would suddenly reveal the goblin or that he would have travelled back to the Kingdom? Of course it would not, the clock told him that it was twenty-two minutes to seven and this to Tommy was a cue to get back into bed. Who in their right mind was up at twenty-two minutes to seven on a Sunday morning?

"Tommy, are you awake?" There came a quiet tap on his door. It was Martha and she gently opened the door and peered toward Tommy. "It's a quarter to nine and we could really do with setting off before ten." Tommy sat bolt upright.

"Where are we going?" A quarter to nine, where had the last two hours gone? Martha came into the room and sat gently on the edge of the bed.

"Don't you remember dear? We're going to Stonehenge and we're going to have a picnic. Clarissa and Tiffany are coming with us. Are you feeling all right sweetheart?" she put her hand to his forehead to see if he had a temperature.

The memory of this trip had been carefully obliterated from his mind and he had been quite meticulous in doing this. Now, however the true feeling of reluctance flooded back and he nodded slowly.

"I won't be long," he said and slid out of the other side of the bed. Martha smiled to herself, Tommy had obviously been very deeply asleep and she had woken him just in time. Tommy grabbed his underwear and headed into the bathroom for a hot bath. Strangely there was no one in there, so he quickly bathed, cleaned his teeth and slipped on his underwear. As he emerged, Clarissa squealed,

"Oh that's gross. Put some clothes on before Tiff gets here." Tommy hadn't even contemplated the fact that there might be girls wandering about and in a most embarrassed fashion he beat a hasty retreat back to his room.

As he tied up his shoe laces, Tommy heard the doorbell ring and Clarissa sped down the stairs. That would be Tiffany then. He looked at his alarm clock and it told him that it was twelve minutes to ten. He was most impressed with himself, he wasn't even going to get into trouble for being late. At the bottom of the stairs he was nearly knocked over by Martha.

"Has the picnic arrived yet?" she enquired. Tommy did not understand the question.

"Where from?" he asked and hastily stepped back onto the second step.

"Emily's of course, it's the only place around here that you can trust to put together a decent picnic." Tommy sat down on the second step and waited patiently. He did not understand what was happening just now. When he and his Mum and Dad had gone for a picnic, his mother had stood for hours the night before preparing sandwiches, sausage rolls and chicken legs. To have one delivered was not something he was at all comfortable with.

"Out of the way Shorty." Clarissa and Tiffany were coming down the stairs with goodness knows how much luggage stuffed into two massive bags. Tommy looked at these bags and wondered what exactly he had missed. Just then his Dad went past.

"Dad?" David hesitated, unsure whether to follow Martha in her panic around the arrival of picnics or to reassure his son that everything was going well.

"Yes Tommy?" he had obviously decided to speak to Tommy.

"Why have they got so much stuff?" he pointed at Clarissa and Tiffany as they disappeared through the front door. David smiled.

"That's women for you Tommy. They don't need most of it, they just think they do." Tommy nodded, his father was reassuring, but what on earth had they got in those bags?

"David!" Martha shouted from the kitchen. This was not normal for her, she was normally quite a calm person. Tommy sat down again on the stairs, when they wanted him he was sure they would call him. Until then he felt safer out of the way and not involved in what was turning into a major military operation.

Presently David and Martha passed him, David carrying a hamper that had obviously arrived and Martha desperately checking the contents of her handbag. Neither of them seemed to notice him until he spoke.

"Are we going now Dad?" he asked and both adults stopped abruptly.

"Why aren't you in the car?" asked Martha. Tommy didn't like the look on her face and he immediately sprinted out to join the others. This enjoying yourself lark really required a lot of effort and self control. Tommy wasn't sure he was up to it really.

In the car, Clarissa mostly ignored him and chatted to Tiffany about some bloke whom they both thought was worthy of their attention. David and Martha seemed intent on desperately 'enjoying' the day and so he dozed quietly in the corner until they reached their destination.

"Come on Shorty." Clarissa shoved Tommy out of the back of the BMW as she dragged her huge bag with her. Tommy stumbled out and turned to help her. He grabbed the end of her bag and struggled under the weight of it, what on earth was in it he had no idea.

"Well, don't offer to help me will you?" Tommy grimaced at Tiffany's piercing voice and bent back into the car to help her with her bag.

"Good man," said his father who happened to pass him, helping Martha with her bag. Tommy was pleased that his father had praised him but he was not sure that he wanted any from Tiffany or from Clarissa. He wanted somewhere that was quiet, where he could contemplate the happenings of the previous night. He felt as though there was something he had to do, or something that he had forgotten but he could not remember what it was.

They had soon arrived at Stonehenge, the roads had been quite clear of heavy traffic. David and Martha began to organise the picnic whilst Tommy, Clarissa and Tiffany decided to check out the area.

"I don't believe it. Old Ravensface is here." Tommy's heart sank. It was the voice of Rick Priestly, the leader of the gang that were bullying him at school. "What a big fat mummy's boy, helping the ladies with their luggage." Tommy turned around and saw to his dismay that not only Rick Priestly, but Dave Mounter and Ian Robertson were standing behind him. All three bullish creatures laughed coarsely and whistled at Tommy.

"Take no notice son," said David. "We'll sort them out when you get back to school. Martha and I are proud of you, you've done really well since you've been here with us, don't spoil it now." Tommy could feel his face going red. He wanted to just curl up and die, but worse was yet to come.

"You don't really know those horrid creatures do you?" squeaked Tiffany. "Where on earth would you meet things like that?"

"At school," muttered Tommy, slamming the car door and rushing after his father.

"What on earth are you related to?" Tiffany whispered to Clarissa, who gave her such a foul look that she immediately fell silent. Clarissa sneaked a look at these boys, they most certainly were not her idea of acceptable classmates and she was glad they did not attend her school. Maybe he was being bullied and maybe he did need help. He hadn't struck her as a wimp and these boys really were most unpleasant. Tiffany started to feel quite uncomfortable as they walked, this was not the first time that Clarissa had supported Tommy and it was she who now began to feel like an outsider.

Presently they came to a picnic spot and David heaved the massive hamper onto one of the tables. Tommy heaved a sigh of relief, maybe he could sneak off on his own for a while. Tiffany and Clarissa plonked down their bags and began to rummage inside them.

"If it was summer, we could sunbathe," Tiffany whined. "Why have we come here to look at some old stones?" Martha looked at David, but before either of them could speak Tommy spoke.

"Those 'old stones' as you call them have been there for thousands of years. They were not erected by machines, they were brought here for a purpose and even if we don't understand it, we should at least respect them." With that, he plonked himself down at the picnic table.

"Can I help?" he asked Martha. The entire party stared at Tommy; this was not what they had expected from him. They had all to some degree expected it to be him with a problem of coming to look at an ancient monument when he would really rather be at home with his mother.

Tiffany blushed and hung her head. Clarissa wasn't sure if she wanted Tommy or Tiffany to disappear but she felt most uncomfortable and looked at her mother for reassurance. Martha was looking at David, who smiled and put his arm around her. Clarissa felt entirely alone, this was not something she warmed to and she gestured to Tiffany to follow her. They left the table, leaving bags and contents unattended and they went up the hill and whispered together. Tommy turned to his Dad.

"May I go and look at the stones?" he asked. This would give him an opportunity to be alone more than anything and he would be able to think about things.

"Don't be long son. Martha is serving lunch at twelve thirty so you have exactly one hour." Tommy looked at his watch and nodded. He skipped off and went in the direction of the standing stones. True there was a cordon around them but all the same he wanted to be on his own right now and that was the only place that sprang immediately to mind.

As he walked he considered both last night and today. Both were challenging but for entirely different reasons. The cordon on this occasion was not supervised and he sneaked carefully under the barrier. The stones stood like age-old centuries surveying the horizon. They were massive in stature and Tommy felt very small and insignificant by comparison. As he approached the one nearest him, it seemed to draw him closer and he felt the same uncomfortable power that he had about the grandfather clock back at the house. As he approached the fallen stone he was compelled to speak.

"Hello? Is someone there?" A strange shadow seemed to pass over the whole field and Tommy shivered even though there was no cold breeze. As quickly as it had arrived, the feeling left him and he was free to survey the stone.

Slowly he held out his left hand and touched the surface of the fallen stone, for some reason it was not cold. The weather was quite mild for October, yet Tommy had expected the stone to be quite cool to touch. As he felt the surface beneath his hand he had a flashback from his dream, or was it from the visions he had in the house? The suspended door appeared in front of him and then immediately vanished again. Tommy felt quite wobbly and leaned on the stone by his side. As he felt the surface he became aware of markings along the edge. They appeared to be some sort of inscription and forgetting his other worry he bent down to read whatever written was there.

His mouth went dry and his hand began to shake as he read the letters. He could definitely see an 'F', an 'L', then he was sure it was an 'I' and what looked like a 'V'. The edge of the rock was then quite jagged, but to him the name was quite clear: 'Fliw'. Tommy quickly stood up and then rested on the stone for support. It hadn't been a dream it had all been quite real. He needed help and he needed it fast, but who would believe him? The grown-ups surely wouldn't, his only chance was Clarissa. This was a real problem; she was currently away with Tiffany doing whatever it is that girls do and not even remotely interested in Tommy's dreams.

"Tommy, help!" Tommy was suddenly aware that he could hear his name and it was Clarissa who called him. He quickly tried to locate the sound and soon pin-pointed it somewhere to his right and further up into the trees. Immediately he left the stones and the inscription and went in search of the problem.

Turning the corner at breakneck speed Tommy found the source of the problem. It was Rick Priestly and his crew and they were tormenting Clarissa and Tiffany. Rick was holding Tiffany by the ear and Dave Mounter was holding Clarissa by her plaits. Ian Robertson was threatening them both with a nasty worm skewered on the end of a stick.

"Let's see if he comes to rescue you then shall we?" spat Rick at Tiffany.

"He's nothing to do with me," whimpered Tiffany, "He's her half-brother, not mine." Rick enjoyed this.

"So he's not even part of a proper family? Oh this just gets better and better chaps, don't you think?" All three of them nodded and laughed.

"Don't you dare," spat Clarissa. "He's far better than any of you lot any day." Tommy was quite shocked at this. He had not thought that Clarissa even liked him and here she was defending him. He had to do something and he had to do it fast.

As he stood there, trembling and thinking what to do, he imagined all three of them falling over and rolling in the thick red mud at their feet. This image became stronger as the two girls squealed louder at their torment, Tommy closed his eyes and commanded them to let go. Suddenly everything went quiet and Tommy opened his eyes. To his amazement the boys had let go of the girls and were all looking at him. This was not good, he could not possibly fight all three of them and he was sure this

105

was going to turn out badly.

"Quick," he shouted to the girls. "You go and find Dad and Martha." They needed no encouragement and were soon scuttling away behind Tommy. The three boys hesitated and looked at Tommy who turned on his heels and fled in the same direction as the girls. He could hear their shouts behind him and assumed that they were in hot pursuit, however as they had not caught up with him he slowed and turned to see what had happened.

Tommy stopped in his tracks. The boys were not following him at all. In fact they had not moved more than one or two metres before they had slid over in the mud and were currently wrestling with each other in an attempt to stand. Tommy stood and laughed out loud and then he turned to join the others.

On the way home in the car Tommy had a lot to think about. He contemplated the inscription on the stone and how Clarissa had supported him against the bullies and then about how his wish for them to get muddy had actually happened. In all, the day had been most peculiar and Tommy was quite unsettled by the whole thing.

Chapter 10

Sunday night soon came around. Tommy was still undecided about his trip to the Kingdom. 'Was it real or was it a dream?' Wilf had visited and explained the history surrounding the house and pointed out its dim and distant ties with mysterious events. The most unbelievable part of his story was that Tommy himself was some sort of saviour of the universe. It must be a dream – but what a dream!

'I wonder if Hoy-Paloy will come again tonight,' he thought. Midnight was approaching, it would not be too long to wait. His eyes began to roll with tiredness in an attempt to keep awake. Soon Tommy was in a deep sleep, his head face down on the pillow, totally unaware of the grandfather clock striking midnight.

Eight, nine, ten, eleven…

"Hoy-Paloy is on his way.

He has a task to do this day.

Fliw the mystic made me this charm.

The purpose of which is to keep us from harm.

Pretty flowers and forests too.

Can we save them? Tommy, its up to you."

Out of the darkness the figure of Hoy-Paloy began to materialise. Tommy was aware of this by now and he was wide-awake, kneeling in an upright position on the bed.

"Hoy-Paloy, you're back."

"Of course I am. Did you think I was a fictitious person? I've come to collect you, Fliw is waiting to start your training."

"Oh right, OK!" Hoy-Paloy walked right past him and onto the landing. Tommy followed obediently to the grandfather clock, patiently waiting for Hoy-Paloy to turn the golden key. It clicked with precision within the lock and once again the doorway appeared into the Kingdom. The cave (or rather home) looked exactly the same as before. What had not occurred to Tommy was that it was a world without television, or computers and play stations.

"Phew," he sighed.

"What did you say Tommy?"

"Oh nothing, just deep in thought," Tommy replied. They followed the same route to Fliw's house, down the path and through the woods. However this time Tommy felt a little uneasy, those warning bells began to alert him of imminent danger.

"And where do you think you're going?" a voice squawked.

"Oh no! It's Miss Tonge, she's followed me here." Tommy instinctively yelled.

"That's Schwartzkopf the witch. Quick Tommy, hide. Follow me." Hoy-Paloy fled at the speed of light and disappeared into a small hollow at the bottom of the valley. Tommy's head span in the direction of the voice.

"And the hermit thinks you will be able to save the Kingdom – Ha ha ha. You puny little urchin I'll swat you like a fly." By now, he was getting desperate. There was a voice but to whom it belonged there was no sign. Panic began to strike, he was on his own in a strange land and being threatened – this shouldn't happen to an eleven-year-old boy.

It was a puff of smoke that followed the loud bang and both made Tommy jump with surprise. It was a classic entrance for a witch. There, as large as life stood a hideous ugly looking witch dressed in black with the biggest nose anyone had ever seen. The sight of the witch before him could not be fully described, simply because there weren't, according to Tommy, enough bad words in the dictionary.

The sight that greeted him posed a clear threat, what would happen now? How would Tommy handle it? The witch approached him, he was unable to move, as if his feet were welded to the ground. The thought of running occurred to him but his legs felt like jelly and would be useless if he tried. Schwartzkopf was by this time strutting around Tommy tutting and laughing at the child before her.

"Oh how pitiful, I don't know whether to turn you into a pig or banish you to another dimension for eternity – which would you prefer?"

"Neither," replied Tommy. "They both sound awful and anyhow my Mum and Dad wouldn't like it." His reply dumbfounded her for a few moments, expecting him to either cower in terror or run as Hoy-Paloy had done.

"So be it! I've decided it will be pig's trotters for dinner tonight." From inside her long black cape emerged a familiar black stick, which was slowly raised above her head. Tommy's eyes, fully expecting the worst, followed the ominous gesture.

'Oh well,' he thought 'it looks like a pig's life – however short for me.' His eyes closed expecting that in an instant he would be snorting, not speaking when…

"Fliw to the rescue." It was Hoy-Paloy's voice. Tommy's eyes opened to see that standing in front of Schwartzkopf was Fliw the Hermit.

"You!" she screeched "Your days are numbered." From the end of her stick shot a lightning bolt directed at Tommy. Fliw raised his left arm and blocked the lightning bolt with an invisible shield. A second and third followed, again towards Tommy. Again an invisible shield appeared and shrouded Tommy, absorbing their energy.

"Wow, how did you do that?" he shouted in absolute amazement. Fliw concentrated on the situation in front of him, not allowing his mind to wander from his mission. Schwartzkopf once again raised her stick. This time the gesture was different and from its head came a dense fog that surrounded Fliw with its acrid stench. The poisonous fog disappeared as quickly as it had appeared with a further gesture from Fliw's right hand.

The situation was clearly getting to an impasse and Schwartzkopf was beginning to realise this and became frustrated.

"'Till another day Fliw, and that day will be your last." Schwartzkopf uttered a small chant and disappeared in a flash.

"And now you've met Schwartzkopf the witch and right hand man of The Something," said Hoy-Paloy. "Between them is the threat that is real to both our worlds. I ran for help knowing that only Fliw could help us and from what I could see he was just in time." Suddenly behind Tommy came a deep thud. Fliw had fallen to his knees exhausted by the use of his powers.

"Fliw, are you all right, are you injured?" Tommy was concerned about the hermit who was kneeled before him.

"I am all right, just let me have a few seconds to recover. Each time this happens and I'm forced to use my powers I get weaker. Because of my age it takes longer for me to fully recover; in fact that function is down to you. With your help, between us we should rectify the situation and restore the balance between our worlds. Come Tommy, let us return to my home and begin your training."

Fliw staggered along aided by his stick and refusing

help from Hoy-Paloy and Tommy. The sight of Fliw's home was like a sanctuary to the trio.

"Don't worry once we are inside, neither Schwartzkopf the witch or The Something will be able to harm us." Fliw was true to his word; inside the fear soon disappeared. "And now for your training Tommy. You need to remember one simple rule – that an Arch Druid's power is in his mind. They require no sticks or gimmicks or enchantments, just the power of the mind."

"You mean I just think it and it happens?"

"Well, yes and no!"

"Now I'm confused. What do you mean by yes and no?"

"Simply, yes you think it however the thoughts must only be defensive and protective they must never injure the innocent. Your thoughts have to be clear and concentrated, any break in the pattern will cancel the deed."

"Erm, yes OK. I mean, I think I understand."

"Your powers need to be exercised to maximise their strength. This will only happen given time. However the most important job is to maintain the integrity of the gateway. This is achieved by concentrated thought only, and it has to be sustained concentrated thought. Do you understand Tommy? Nothing must distract you from this fundamental duty, the entire…"

"Yes, yes, existence of the universe including your world and mine are in my hands."

"Don't be flippant, you forget I'm the master and you the apprentice. Don't take the situation lightly, we depend on one another."

"Yes sorry Fliw, but I'm only eleven-years-old. You forget." For the next few hours Tommy was given secret mental exercises only known to Druids and mystics. From what he managed to glean at first from Fliw the powers within him included some form of telekinesis, levitation, invisibility and a power to create an invisible shield. Something else was said around the ability to control nature and its forces. The best bit was that the powers were unlimited and could extend further than those known to Fliw. This eleven year-old boy was quickly growing up.

Tommy practised for hours and remembered the time rule in the Kingdom. He didn't want David and Martha to worry unduly about his absence.

"Right Tommy, it's time for a small test to see if you have learned anything from your studies. Over there behind that stool, is a pot. I want you to levitate yourself to a height of one metre and lift the pot onto the stool. Remember to use the power of your mind and the ancients' legacy invested in you."

Tommy stood squarely in the middle of the room, his eyes concentrating on the stool. His stance reflected his intense mood. After what seemed like minutes, although it was only seconds, Tommy's feet lifted from the floor to the height of a metre. Next the pot lifted from behind the stool. So far, so good. The excitement on his face was beginning to show and that was literally his downfall. The lack of concentration sent the pot careering around the room, just missing Hoy-Paloy and Fliw. It ended in disaster: the pot hit the door and smashed into a thousand pieces. The sight of this disaster and lapse of concentration ended with Tommy tumbling from his levitated position into a heap on the floor.

"Oh darn it!"

Hoy-Paloy chuckled with laughter and Fliw dropped his head into his hands.

"No, no, no. Remember the golden rule is concentration, you will get many distractions but you must focus on what you are trying to achieve. Spend another two hours practising." Tommy diligently continued the mental exercises given to him until Fliw announced it was time to rest.

"You will continue your training here over the next few days, don't forget that time is not passing in your world and therefore your parents will not miss you."

"Thank you Fliw. I don't want Mum and Dad, or Martha, to worry about me."

Over the next few days his training became quite intense. By day two he had mastered levitation and was able to move objects as easily as playing computer games.

"Look at me Fliw." Tommy was floating two metres in the air sitting with his legs crossed and by using telekinesis he balanced Hoy-Paloy underneath him. They both gently floated down to the floor.

"Now, what's next Fliw?"

"The next task is to create an invisible barrier to protect you if necessary from harm, but more important is to form a barrier around the gateway. Now Tommy think of steel plate similar to what they build your ships with in your world. Then imagine it so clear that you may see through, the strength of steel that you can see through. Now Tommy, try!" For the next six hours he tried in vain to do as Fliw asked, but without success. His frustration was apparent in his face, no matter how hard he tried. Tommy just could not master the invisible barrier.

"Never mind Tommy, that's enough for today. It's time to rest. Perhaps day three may show some progress."

"I'm sorry Fliw, I did my best but somehow I just can't get the hang of it. What's on the training schedule for tomorrow?"

"Tomorrow, young man, will be lessons in the power of nature. This will include communication with birds and animals and then moving on to controlling the weather."

"I rather like the idea of talking to the animals, I don't know weather I can change it!" Tommy joked. "Did you get it Fliw, weather and change it?" Fliw looked on in a confused manner completely oblivious to the joke that Tommy had just made.

Night passed quickly and soon birds were singing the dawn chorus. Tommy had become used to the early morning wake up call.

"I'm ready for my next lesson Fliw, when does it begin?"

"It already has. Go outside and look a bird squarely in the eyes and read its mind."

"OK, sounds a little strange to me. No matter, I hope I can do better than yesterday." Tommy went outside. A dozen birds hopped around him singing merrily and pecking at the loose soil for breakfast.

"Mine's a great big juicy one."

"Mine's got a hundred legs."

"Mine got away!" (There had to be one!)

"Don't worry," Tommy whispered. "There's plenty of worms over there."

"Thank you Tommy." And with that the trio scurried off to pastures new.

Next on the scene was a red vixen with her cubs.

"Hello Tommy, how's your training coming along?"

"Oh OK thank you Mrs Fox. Your cubs are so cute."

"Why thank you. Come along children, come along." They disappeared into the forest, when all of a sudden Tommy realised that he had mastered talking to the animals.

"Fliw, Fliw I…"

"Yes, I know Tommy, you made easy work of that task didn't you?"

"That was so easy. What's next? What's next?"

"Don't worry, after breakfast comes another difficult test and that's controlling the elements or the weather." Breakfast was swift, Tommy was so keen to progress further.

"Right what do I do next then?" he enquired.

"Watch me." Fliw raised his hands in a circular motion and seconds later a small breeze passed them by, it appeared to come from nowhere. Within a minute the breeze had turned into a gust reaching gale force proportions and continuing toward storm force and still increasing in intensity. Fliw lowered his hands and everything slowly returned to normal.

"You can control all elements of the weather, again by simply using the power of your mind. Now you try." Copying perfectly Fliw's actions Tommy once again began to concentrate on mimicking the task Fliw had set for him. Minutes passed by with no results.

"Clear your mind Tommy and think only of the task you wish to undertake." Another few minutes passed until again the small breeze appeared, increasing its intensity to gale force and then returning to normal.

"Wow, that was even better."

"Remember Tommy, the need to control the power you have and the fact that you will tire after using your powers."

"I'll remember Fliw, thank you for your concern."

"Now practice again and try to focus the power into smaller areas for greater effect." Tommy did as he was instructed and continued to practice diligently for the next few hours. Fliw coaxed him all the way and taught him to do many more tasks with the power. As the days went by Tommy absorbed the knowledge and lessons Fliw imparted to him. His strength and power increased many fold.

"Right, today," announced Fliw, "we go for invisibility and retry the invisible barrier lesson. You must perfect the barrier as this is the main weapon we will use against The Something. Without an impregnable barrier at the gateway your world is in danger."

"I'll do my best Fliw, but you forget I'm only eleven years-old."

"Yes, but you have the power of an Arch Druid. That makes you a completely different person and one that must take up the challenge. Now to business. Let us retire to the woods."

They wandered past the edge of the forest close to the mountain, talking as they went. Suddenly Fliw stumbled and fell prostrate on the rocky path.

"Fliw are you all right?" a concerned Tommy shouted. He had been following some twenty metres behind Fliw absorbing the beauty and serene environment of the woods. A loud rumble echoed through the trees and there above Fliw a dozen rocks rolled toward the fallen mystic.

"Fliw, the rocks. Look out," warned Tommy, who by now was in full sprint towards Fliw.

"Tommy. Tommy, I'm so weak, my powers... I can't summon enough power to form my invisible shield around us. Go quickly this is the end, go. Go."

"Come on, move." Tommy screamed, heaving the old body from the ground with all the strength he could muster. The rocks tumbled down and grew bigger the closer they came.

"Come. Come on Fliw, move."

"Too weak, can't... too weak." A frail voice replied. "Save yourself, run." Tommy realised that his physical efforts were all in vain, then he wondered, why on earth was he trying to use his strength? He should use his mind.

The rocks were almost upon them, it would be seconds before they were crushed under their weight. Tommy looked up, lips pursed, intense concentration forming on his face. His hands raised toward the rocks now almost upon them. Fliw looked up from the ground and began to raise his own hand, concern showing on his face.

The rocks struck with tremendous force, two tonne boulders travelling at sixty kilometres per hour, no one could survive such an onslaught. The crushing weight danced all around Tommy and Fliw bouncing off an impregnable shield and felling several trees close by.

"You did it, you did it Tommy. Well done. In the face of adversity and danger you managed to form the shield, I knew you could do it." Fliw danced a jig around Tommy slapping him on the back and congratulating him on his achievement.

"Fliw, I thought you had hurt yourself, yet you're dancing. Are you all right?"

"Ah yes, well… erm, yes. I feel better now, shall we move on?" Feeling thoroughly ashamed at the deception he had just played, a red-faced hermit continued walking along the path knowing that he had created the situation to test Tommy with positive results. There had not really been any danger, the thought created rocks were only virtual, had they struck either of them they would have been harmless.

"I did it! I did it! Thanks to you Fliw."

"I always knew you could Tommy, it just takes a little time and practice, practice. Next, whilst you continue to form protective shields, I want you to try the power of invisibility. Now concentrate again and will yourself to disappear just like this." Before Tommy's eyes, Fliw gradually faded away, however he continued to speak and to encourage Tommy to follow him.

"Now it's your turn Tommy. Concentrate," he obeyed the command and gradually one leg faded, then two legs and an arm, his torso and eventually his head disappeared.

"There. What an achievement, you've done it first time, now stop concentrating and hey presto you're visible again. One thing to remember with invisibility, you can't walk through solid walls. If you try, you're in for a shock."

It was another two more days into Tommy's training programme before Fliw announced he had taught as much as he could. The strain on Fliw was now visible; the intense training schedule had clearly taken its toll on the old man. Unawares to Tommy, though Fliw could feel the force, The Something was growing. For once in his own lifetime Fliw began to think that his own power was insufficient to keep The Something in check and he looked extremely worried.

"It's time for you to return to your own world Tommy. You need to see your family – after all, as you continually remind me, you are only eleven years-old. I've called for Hoy-Paloy to escort you to the gateway and he should be here any…" There was a loud knock at the door and in marched Hoy-Paloy.

"One passenger to be delivered through the gateway," he jested. Tommy waved goodbye to Fliw and followed Hoy-Paloy back along the path toward the cave.

He removed the two golden keys from the invisible box and placed them around his neck.

"Are you ready Tommy?"

"Sure am. Let's go," Tommy answered. Hoy-Paloy placed the large key in the lock and they both disappeared. Seconds later the two travellers reappeared through the fireplace in Tommy's bedroom.

"I'll be leaving you now Tommy, see you tomorrow night at the same time." Hoy-Paloy left the bedroom, inserted the small key into the grandfather clock and disappeared back into The Kingdom. Tommy yawned, quickly washed and brushed his teeth and went to bed.

Hoy-Paloy soon rejoined Fliw at his cabin. He had already assembled Twinkle, Casey and Brett, but as Hoy-Paloy entered the room the mood appeared sombre and the huge grin on his face soon disappeared. He realised all his friends were standing around Fliw. The look on his face was one of concern.

"What's the matter?"

"It's serious," replied Twinkle "Fliw is very weak and we feel that the last ten days have drained his powers to a critical level."

"Darn sure 'bout that," interrupted Casey. "We suspect the time is very close and Fliw will not have enough strength to protect the gateway."

"Stop." Fliw once more took control of the conversation. "My powers may be weak but I have to maintain that gateway at all costs. Tommy may not yet be prepared to take on his full responsibilities. His training went perfectly but the task he must undertake will stretch him to the limit."

The worried look on so many faces described the situation perfectly. What would under normal circumstances be a group of happy, carefree characters was no more. Gradually they all left the house and Hoy-Paloy returned to check that the keys in the invisible box were safe and the gateway was intact. The only one that remained was Twinkle and she felt she knew the perfect remedy to this quandary. It was a cup of tea and a piece of cake.

Chapter 11

Tommy rolled over and pulled the duvet over his head. Why couldn't someone just turn off that alarm? It had been ringing for ages now and no one seemed to be doing anything about it. How he hated alarm clocks, you needed them to get you up and yet when they went off it was the worst thing in the history of the world. Slowly the ringing seeped through the barrier of duck down and Tommy could hear it again quite clearly. He stuck his head from under the cover. It was still dark and there was not even a hint of daylight sneaking through the gap in the curtains of his bedroom. Slowly it dawned on him that the alarm clock was in fact his and it was he who should switch it off. He stuck his arm out and slammed his hand over the button on the top of the clock. Suddenly everything returned to silence.

Tommy breathed a sigh of relief and fell back on the pillow with his eyes closed. He'd had the most outrageous dream again last night. He had dreamt that there had been someone or something in his room and again they had travelled to a world that didn't exist. He had met the hermit again who was an exact replica of Wilf the librarian. Hold on. Tommy's eyes snapped open, there was no way he had dreamt that and it had really happened. He reached his hand over to the bedside light and snapped it on, the soft yellow light illuminated the room a little. Tommy quickly searched the room for evidence of last night's adventure, but to no avail. He could not see any evidence at all of strange worlds where there were two suns and three moons. Maybe he had dreamt it after all. He lay back and contemplated this dream. He had been so sure he was really there. Anyway it had been two nights in a row, maybe he was going round the bend.

Suddenly the door burst open and in came Clarissa, still in her nightie.

"Oh good. You're awake, hurry up and get washed and dressed, we're leaving in twenty minutes."

"What?" Tommy didn't understand. "Leaving for where?" Clarissa stood with her hand on her hip and tapped her slippered foot impatiently.

"We're going to Alton Towers, dummy. Don't you remember?" Tommy felt the memory come flooding back. This meant that it was just after six o'clock in the morning. He groaned at the prospect of having to be vertical at this time of day. Clarissa's face suddenly changed and her nose wrinkled as she looked at the side of Tommy's bed. "Oh good grief. You are going to be in so much trouble. What have you been doing in the night? Have you been sleepwalking out in the garden or what?" With that, she turned and flounced out of the door, slamming it quite sharply behind her.

Tommy hadn't understood a word of what she had just said, so he peered tentatively over the side of the bed. To his amazement, on the floor by the side of the bed were his slippers and suddenly the memory came flooding back. He had definitely gone with Hoy-Paloy through the door in the clock and had entered the other world through Hoy-Paloy's home. Outside the cave in which he lived there had been quite a distinctly reddish muddy patch through which they had walked. To Tommy's initial dismay and then sudden excitement he noticed that his slippers were covered in the same reddish coloured mud. Unfortunately the mud also seemed to have rubbed off a little on the carpet. At least it meant that he really had been to the other place and it hadn't all just been a dream.

In a blind panic, Tommy leapt up and cleaned his slippers and did his very best at cleaning the carpet, to make sure that no one could reprimand him for making a mess. Then he rushed to shower and get dressed. Today they were going to Alton Towers and they had to set off very early, otherwise they'd hit all the queues and have to wait to go on any of the rides. Half of him wanted to try and get back to Hoy-Paloy and the other half was desperate to go and ride the attractions at Alton Towers. Somewhere along the line, he showered, cleaned his teeth, got dressed and brushed his hair. Almost as soon as he had finished, Clarissa was back. The door flew open and she stood there wearing Calvin Klein jeans and a DKNY sweatshirt. It occurred to Tommy that she was most probably the most fashion conscious person he knew.

"Ready yet Shorty?" she looked straight at the place where his slippers had been. "At least you've tidied up a bit," Clarissa snorted.

"I thought you'd stopped calling me Shorty. I'm ready when you are," he heaved a sigh of relief, he was only just ready and he wasn't sure that he'd cleaned off all of the mud from the carpet or from his slippers. His jeans and sweatshirt were from the supermarket where his mum shopped and he felt suddenly conscious that he hadn't got designer labels. Was this day going to be a success or was he going to feel like an outcast?

Chapter 12

They all met downstairs in the hallway.

"Marvellous," announced Martha. "Well done you two, you've managed to get yourselves ready in plenty of time. We just need to get the picnic into the car and we're away. Tommy," she turned in his direction "can you get the basket from the kitchen?" Tommy trotted off obediently to find the basket. He wandered into the kitchen, but could not find the basket anywhere. But what he did find were tiny footprints in the reddish mud that he had so hurriedly cleaned out of his bedroom. He stood and looked at the footprints for a while, suddenly Clarissa appeared at the door.

"What's taking so long Shorty?" she asked. "We're all waiting for you."

"Don't call me Shorty," he snapped, and Clarissa joined him in the investigation of the little footprints.

"You know something about this don't you?" she asked.

"You wouldn't believe me if I tried to tell you," he responded.

"So there is something going on then?" she persisted. Tommy nodded, but Martha interrupted them.

"Where is the picnic hamper I ordered?" she enquired.

"It doesn't seem to have arrived Mummy," replied Clarissa. Martha sighed rather heavily.

"What on earth do we do now then?" she began to panic, but Clarissa leapt in, much to Tommy's amazement.

"Mummy, if you and David go and have something nice to eat in the restaurant, Tommy and I will go and find a hamburger or something. What do you think Tommy? You and I need to talk about stuff anyway, don't we?" Tommy nodded in resignation. Those had definitely been Hoy-Paloy's footprints and obviously he had found the picnic most enticing.

Martha nodded in resignation, she could think of no other solution to their predicament. Clarissa was happy because she could interrogate Tommy and Tommy was relieved because he did not have to answer for the ridiculous disappearance of the picnic hamper. Consequently they all climbed into David's dark blue BMW car that had been parked at the front of the house. As the last door slammed, Tommy's father spoke.

"So. What are we eating at lunch time then?" The two children looked out of their respective windows in the back of the car and pretended that they had not heard the question. Martha said.

"Apparently, the hamper hasn't arrived, so we're to eat by ourselves whilst the children entertain themselves with fast food and the like." David looked at her quizzically, but she offered no further explanation.

"OK," he responded. "Let's be gone." And off they drove. Martha puzzled as to why the hamper she had ordered had not been delivered. David was confused because he could feel that something was not quite right with either Martha or with Tommy. Clarissa was desperate to know how the reddish mud had appeared both in Tommy's room and in the kitchen. Tommy, well Tommy was desperately trying to work out what exactly had happened last night. In accordance with most family outings, no one wanted to ask the first question and so they drove in absolute quiet for a few miles. A news bulletin on the radio broke the silence. Several crop circles had mysteriously appeared in the fields surrounding Alton Towers. The news announcer explained that no one understood their meaning or how they were constructed. Wild claims had been made that it could be aliens visiting from another world, but no evidence could be provided.

Clarissa nudged Tommy. "So?"

Tommy looked at her. It was still around seven in the morning and in his holidays this time officially did not exist.

"So what?" he responded. She shot him a most annoyed look and then turned away from him and spent the rest of the journey with her back to Tommy.

Tommy was exhausted and curled up in his corner and wrapped himself in his coat. He slept most of the way up the motorway and dreamed the same dreams as he had the previous night. He dreamt that he had been with Hoy-Paloy and with Fliw, all of this confused him and he was almost relieved when they arrived at Alton Towers.

"Tommy, come on son. Are you with us?" David was speaking to him now. "Tommy." Tommy sat bolt upright and looked about him. Then he looked at his watch, it was nearly ten o'clock. The feeling of drowsiness had not left him and he forced his eyes open. As he looked round, he could see many other cars on either side. They were in a massive car park and had obviously arrived at Alton Towers.

"Come on Tommy," said Martha. "Don't miss anything, it'll be ages before we can come again." Tommy desperately tried to regain some sort of consciousness and decided that if he could get himself out of the car and follow them for a while, then they might leave him alone.

As they walked across the car park, Clarissa turned to him and whispered, "What were you doing last night?"

Tommy thought deeply about this and replied, "Sleeping. Or rather trying to sleep."

Clarissa seemed more intrigued, "And?"

"And what?" Tommy was struggling to put one foot in front of the other. Also he was lamenting the fact that he had been roused at some unearthly hour in order to be a party to this family trip.

"And what exactly did you do instead?" Tommy shook his head and caught up with his dad. He took hold of his father's hand and the four of them entered the theme park together.

Once inside, Clarissa immediately asked,

"Mummy, may Tommy and I go and see if they've opened the new ride?" Martha looked quickly at David.

"What do you think, dear?" she asked, the whole event to her had already been a disaster and she was desperately looking for some sort of reassurance.

"Oh, I can't think why not," he looked at his watch. "You meet us here at the entrance at exactly twelve thirty and we'll all have lunch together," he reached into his back pocket. "Here's a ten pound note each for ice creams and things." He passed one each to the children. "Go and enjoy yourselves but don't get into any trouble. Be back here at twelve thirty prompt and we'll have something to eat. OK?"

Both children nodded eagerly. To be a teenager, well almost, and be free of your parents at Alton Towers is not an opportunity to be missed.

As they dashed away, Clarissa turned to Tommy.

"You've got an awful lot of explaining to do young man." Tommy laughed.

"You sound just like my teacher from school," he responded. Clarissa didn't laugh, but shot him an evil look.

"Where were you last night? What happened to the hamper and why on earth are you so tired?" Tommy tried to laugh it all off.

"Why do you want to know?" he sneered.

"Because there's something happening that I don't know about around here."

"You wouldn't believe me if I told you," he responded, and they walked along in a most frightful silence. Both of them were determined not to back down.

"Do you fancy the ghost train?" asked Clarissa. "Or are you too scared?" This was like a red rag to a bull for Tommy.

"Of course I'm not scared, I'll bet you scream before I do." As they rounded the first corner Clarissa let out a yell.

"Ha. Too late I've spotted one. Over there, it's massive. We'll soon see exactly how brave you are Thomas Ravensdale." They raced to the entrance, and strangely there was no queue for this ride. Within a matter of seconds they were seated in the car and strapped into their seats. Clarissa fingered the strong bar that held them down.

"You don't think we really need these do you?" she asked nervously. Tommy tried to smile reassuringly, but he wasn't entirely convinced himself.

After a few more seconds, the car jerked forward and they were on their way.

"Too late to get off now anyway," shrugged Tommy and took a deep breath. It surely could not be that terrible, could it? As they entered the tunnel, everything went black and Clarissa grabbed hold of Tommy's arm. Tommy didn't pull away and they continued steadily on their way. Strange things dragged across their faces and Tommy laughed as Clarissa screamed out loud. This is what was supposed to happen in ghost trains, after all. He thought it was amusing that Clarissa was so scared.

They saw strange creatures and heard weird noises and smelled all kinds of horrid smells. Suddenly, the car ground to a halt. Clarissa had buried her head in Tommy's sweatshirt and slowly peered around the edge.

"Tommy?" she whispered. "Is this supposed to happen?"

"I don't know," he whispered back. His voice was a little shaky also, but he tried to reassure her. "They'll notice soon and come and start it up again." Clarissa nodded, of course that was the most likely thing that would happen. Yet, she still didn't let go of Tommy and she seemed to grip even harder. Through the dark, Tommy tried to see if he could identify a door or the exit somewhere. Surely they could not be very far from the end of the ride, they had been on it for quite a while. Slowly he became aware of a cool breeze on the left of his face. All of the hairs on his arms stood on end. This was the same coolness he felt when The Something was around. It could not possibly have followed him here could it? Clarissa felt his arm tense.

"What is it?" she whispered so quietly that Tommy could hardly hear her.

"I'm not sure. Can you see anything over to the left?" As they strained to see anything at all, they became aware of a movement to their left. The outline was not distinct and neither one of them could tell what colour they were looking toward. Slowly, the movement came closer. Tommy spoke making Clarissa jump.

"Not here. Be gone, I want nothing to do with you." Clarissa stared in amazement as the 'whatever it was' disappeared into thin air. She sat open mouthed as Tommy rubbed his eyes and tried to see where it had gone.

Suddenly the car jerked forward again and within a few minutes the ride was over.

"Sorry," yelled the assistant as they got off the ride. "We must have had some sort of power cut for a few seconds. Hope it didn't spoil your fun." The two of them dashed over to an ice cream stall and bought themselves an ice cream each. It seemed Clarissa no longer wanted to talk about what had happened. This was much to Tommy's relief, as he really had no idea what he should say to her. He felt a small knot of fear developing in the pit of his stomach. It seemed that he could no longer get away from The Something.

"Come on," cried Clarissa. "Time's running out, if we're not careful we won't be able to do everything before we have to be back." Both children ran from ride to ride enjoying the wonderful atmosphere of Alton Towers.

"It's only just about twelve o'clock," said Tommy looking at his watch "We don't have to be back until twelve thirty." Clarissa nodded in agreement.

"We might as well go and wait for them anyway. They may be there early." It took them quite a while to get from one end of the theme park to the other, as the attraction was becoming quite busy. They were both making mental notes as to which rides they would vote for first after lunch.

"There they are," said Tommy. "We've caught up with them just before they've arrived themselves."

"Mummy," shouted Clarissa, and Martha and David both turned around and waved.

"Well done you two," said David. "We had a feeling that we would be waiting here for quite a while."

"We ran out of money," said Tommy. David and Martha both laughed out loud.

"So are you having a good time?" asked Martha,

thinking that maybe the day wasn't going to be a disaster after all. Both children nodded. "Let's sit here a while and hear all about it. When it gets to twelve thirty, we can all go to the restaurant and eat together." Tommy slid Clarissa a quick look, but she didn't seem to be concerned that they would all eat together. Maybe she had forgotten that she wanted to interrogate him. They all sat on a park bench and Clarissa began to tell the tale about the ghost train.

"When we went on the ghost train, it was really scary. The lights went out and the ride stopped for ages." Martha looked concerned.

"What happened? How did you get off?"

Tommy slid Clarissa a warning stare, but she continued.

"Well, Tommy said that they would notice and that someone would come and get us out." Tommy could feel his mouth going dry. Surely she wasn't going to tell them what really happened? "But it was all over quite quickly and the ride started again. The man said that there must have been a power cut." Tommy heaved a sigh of relief. That had been most uncomfortable.

Clarissa then proceeded to tell Martha and David all about the rest of the rides they had tried. Tommy's mind wandered, he wondered exactly how she could retell every single detail and not let anyone else get a word in edgeways. As his mind wandered, Tommy looked around the park. The sun was shining and it felt as if nothing bad could happen. Maybe he had imagined The Something on the ghost train, it all seemed very dim and distant now. The sun was quite warm on his back and he began to feel a little drowsy again.

Suddenly out of the corner of his eye, he could see something in the sky. There were no other clouds about, just this one semi-transparent little cloud. He looked back at the other three, but they were listening to how he and Clarissa had enjoyed the roller coaster. He snapped his eyes back to the thing in the sky. It was definitely moving and changing shape as it came. No one else seemed to have noticed it, though it seemed to be moving with some sort of purpose. It was not like normal clouds, it had a slight yellow tinge around the edge and it seemed to change shape all the time. Tommy looked to see where its destination might be. It did not appear to be travelling toward him, yet the knot of fear in his stomach began to steadily grow.

He looked round at the sun, to make sure it was still shining. His hands felt very cold and his mouth had gone even drier. He felt the same as he normally did when he was going to sit some sort of test. Why he was nervous, he could not tell, but this cloud-like thing most certainly had something to do with his feelings. Something? Oh, no. It was The Something. Is that what it looked like? He had no idea, he had never seen it face to face, he had only felt its presence. As he followed the direction of travel he could see that the cloud was heading directly for the big roller coaster that Clarissa and he had ridden a few minutes before. There was a car just careering around the bend and heading straight toward The Something. Tommy leapt to his feet and ran to the foot of the ride.

"Stop," he yelled. "Stop the ride, there's something wrong." The operator looked at Tommy and to where he pointed. He could see nothing untoward, but he slowed the car with the emergency brakes.

David, Martha and Clarissa came dashing over to them.

"What is it son?" asked David, putting a reassuring hand on his shoulder.

"Look. Look Dad, can't you see?" They all looked at the car as it slowed toward the hairpin bend directly above the lake. As they watched, Tommy could see the cloud envelop the bend of the track and become steadily thicker. Soon the track began to buckle and as the car approached, the people at the front began to shout at the operator. The operator slammed on the emergency brakes and tried to get the car to travel in reverse. All of them could see the distortion in the tracks and as they watched in horror, the rails began to bend beyond their flexibility. The whole structure began to creak and groan as the stressed metal gave way. Still the car was travelling toward the bend, destined for disaster.

It happened as if in slow motion and the family stood and watched in horror as events unfolded before them. The car hit the snapped rail and left the tracks. The whole car, complete with its passengers, dropped like a stone into the lake. Immediately the emergency procedure was activated and ambulances and security men appeared from everywhere. In the midst of all the chaos, Tommy searched the sky for evidence of The Something. He was convinced he could just make out a distortion on the edge of the skyline.

"Tommy," he suddenly realised that Martha was speaking to him. There was a security man standing next to her. "This man needs to know what you saw dear. Can you tell him?" Everyone was suddenly looking at him.

"Is everyone all right?" he asked. The man smiled and nodded.

"Thanks to you, the car had nearly stopped and fell straight into the lake. No one was killed or injured, although several people are going to hospital to be treated for shock and some swallowed quite a lot of water." Tommy heaved a massive sigh of relief, they all did. That would have really ruined the day. The man was speaking again, he took off his security hat and crouched down. Tommy thought he looked rather like a policeman with his navy trousers and blue shirt.

"Can you tell me what happened son?" Tommy opened and closed his mouth several times before he carefully chose his words.

"Well," Clarissa sniggered but soon stopped as David gave her a reproachful glance. "I looked up and I could see something on the end of the bend. It was bending the tracks and it looked as if the car would fly right off the end and into the people down here." The man nodded.

"That's right son. If you hadn't told someone, that's exactly what would have happened. Now what did you see? No one else saw anything." Tommy struggled to find the right words but eventually shrugged.

"I don't know. There was definitely something there but I don't honestly know what it was." The security man smiled and stood up again. He put on his hat and ruffled Tommy's hair.

"Well, no matter. At least you saved everyone from something terrible."

"Yes. The Something is terrible," Tommy muttered to himself.

"Sorry, son. What did you say?"

"I said 'Thank Goodness it wasn't something terrible'." The security man smiled and nodded to Martha and David. Then he turned and went off to organise whatever it is that security men organise. Martha grabbed hold of Tommy.

"Tommy, that was so brave. If you hadn't done that, so many people would have been really badly hurt." She gave Tommy the biggest hug. Tommy struggled to breathe and tried not to let the shock show on his face. His father patted him on the back.

"Nice one Tommy. We'll have to remember to bring you with us wherever we go." Tommy could just see Clarissa's face over Martha's shoulder. He thought she would be cross at the attention he was getting from both of the adults. Her face did not show it, she was grinning widely and he knew she was laughing at him. She was acutely aware that Tommy was not impressed by public displays of emotion and this must be the most embarrassing situation in which he had ever been.

After a while David spoke again.

"I think we've all had rather too much excitement for one day. I suggest we go somewhere closer to home and have a slap-up meal to celebrate Tommy's quick thinking." They all looked at each other. Martha nodded, she wasn't sure how much more excitement she could take. Clarissa smiled at Tommy, but there was something in the expression that warned him that she had not forgotten the interrogation she had promised him. They all looked at Tommy for his opinion. He sighed and nodded. He felt a little like a fraud. He had seen The Something and yes, he had warned people, but would The Something have been there in the first place if it hadn't been for him? He would never know, but the thought lay heavily on his conscience. They all climbed back into the car and set off for home. Tommy and Clarissa both sat dreaming out of their respective windows for a while and slowly the miles passed away under them.

After around two and a half hours, when they were about an hour from home, David spotted a large pub and restaurant on the side of the road.

"Oh good," he exclaimed. "I'm ravenous, is anyone else hungry?" they all shouted and he flicked on the indicator switch and pulled gently onto the car park. Once they were safely in a parking space, he spoke again. "Right then. You two stay here whilst Martha and I go and see if they have a table for us. We're a bit late for lunch! It's just after five o'clock and not all places serve food all day. Be good and we'll be back in a few minutes." David and Martha got out of the car and went towards the main entrance. Tommy watched them go. He was not sure how he felt and he wasn't sure who he could tell.

"This had better be good." Clarissa made Tommy jump, he had thought she wasn't speaking to him. She had effectively ignored him all the way back down the motorway.

"How do you mean?" he wasn't quite sure whether she would understand. Clarissa snorted in exasperation.

"Look Tommy. I know there's something going on, you've said as much yourself. First you've been up in the night, then someone or something stole the picnic and something has followed us, or you, around all day." Before he could stop himself Tommy responded.

"It's not 'something', it is The Something, and it's a terrible, awful thing. You don't want to get involved in this Clarissa. I'm not sure I want to be involved but I can't seem to get away from the responsibility."

Clarissa looked at Tommy. He had called her by her real name again and he hadn't even noticed. This wimp of a step brother obviously needed her help. Before she could say anything more Martha was at the door of the car.

"Come on," she said, opening the door "They have a table and everything looks lovely." They both climbed out of the back of the car and stretched their stiff limbs. Tommy had never been very good at sitting still and even though he was weighed down with such responsibility he could not resist a good stretch.

The meal was magnificent and they all ate the same.

There were prawns to start, steak and onion rings, and profiteroles to finish. The conversation was kept entirely to the rides the children had ridden and specifically no one mentioned the roller coaster or any of that experience. Soon they were all back in the car and as it went dark the two children dozed pleasantly whilst the adults discussed the implications of the day's events. As they pulled into the driveway, it was a little past seven and Tommy peered at his watch. Clarissa leaned over.

"I've not finished with you yet Tommy. You owe me an explanation." Tommy was puzzled, he didn't owe her anything, but he supposed she would make his life hell if he didn't tell her. He nodded and they leapt out of the car together.

"How on earth have you still got the energy to run around you two?" asked Martha. "I just want a nice hot bath and then I'm ready to settle down for a nice quiet evening." David listened to this and thought that he may have a solution.

"Why don't the two of you go and have a bath and get changed and we'll spend the evening together in the lounge?" Both Tommy and Clarissa pulled a face at the suggestion. David's face changed and broke into a grin.

"Compromise?" he suggested and they both nodded. "If both of you can have a bath and get changed without fighting," he paused until they both nodded. "Then you can stay up and watch television until whatever time you like." They both nodded. "But," he went on. "I don't want to hear a peep out of either of you until morning." They nodded again and went inside.

Martha seemed to have had the worst of the day and she went and had a long hot bath. David took her a cold glass of wine and the two children were left in the kitchen. Clarissa looked at the floor, the small red mud footprints were still visible and Tommy rushed to get a cloth. They both cleaned the floor and removed all trace of the prints. If David or Martha had seen them they would have instantly been suspicious, but they continued uninterrupted.

"OK," said Clarissa, getting them both a can of Coke out of the fridge. "Sit down here," she pulled out a chair "and spill the beans." Tommy did as he was told; he sat down took the drink from Clarissa and looked at her. "Well?" she continued. Tommy couldn't resist.

"Do you have to start every sentence with that word?" Clarissa lost her temper and clipped Tommy around the head.

"Stop it, you moron. You know what I'm talking about, now you'd better tell me what's going on, or I'll tell Mummy that you took the picnic basket." Tommy was stuck with that, he had no way out but to tell her all that he knew.

"When I first came here," he started; Clarissa took a seat opposite him. "I started to see a door." Clarissa nodded.

"You told me."

"Well, the door led into my classroom the first time, but that was in the daytime." Clarissa pulled a face. He continued. "We went to the library and I met a guy called Wilf. He showed me some maps and something was there, something not very nice." His voice trailed away.

"What do you mean 'not very nice'?" Clarissa was slightly scared, but fascinated. This obviously had something to do with their experience today.

"I think I felt it in the library, in Wilf's office. It was cold and hid the sun." He shivered at the thought of the experience. Clarissa put down her can of coke.

"Go on," she prompted.

"Wilf was trying to tell me about The 'Something' and it was really scary, so I ran out of the library and that was when I met you and Tiff on the steps." Clarissa nodded; that bit at least made sense, he had looked as if he had seen a ghost.

"And?"

"Yesterday Wilf came to the house and tried to tell me that I was connected with all this weird stuff." Clarissa looked puzzled.

"You didn't see anyone yesterday," she started, and then she remembered. "That was when I came in with the drinks and biscuits, wasn't it?" Tommy nodded. Clarissa could feel a cold and unwelcome feeling creep all over her body. "What exactly did he tell you?"

"Well." They both pulled faces but decided to let the word go by. "He told me that he was a druid and that I was the 'next in line' sort of thing and then he went. He said I had to battle The Something." Clarissa's eyes widened.

"That was what you said earlier, wasn't it? You said to the security man that it was The Something, but then you changed what you had said." Clarissa slammed down her hand again. "Why didn't you say? It was The Something in the ghost train too, wasn't it? Why didn't you do something about it then?" Clarissa was incensed: she could not believe he had allowed them to be subjected to this.

"What did you want me to do exactly?" Tommy would have half-liked her to give him a credible answer, as far as he was concerned he had no answers.

"Well, kill it. Or send it away, do something. All of those people could have been killed. Why didn't you do something?" Tommy put his head in his hands and wished he was miles and miles away from here.

"What would I have done? I had no idea it could

138

follow me there. Why should it, unless Wilf's story is true?" Clarissa looked at him carefully. She could feel the hairs on the back of her neck standing on end. She decided to change tack.

"So what about the mud on your slippers and the footprints in here?"

"The clock at the top of the stairs?" he gesticulated with his head and Clarissa nodded. "It doesn't strike midnight." Clarissa snorted.

"I know that stupid. It never has."

"Yes, but on the very last strike a person appears." Clarissa laughed out loud.

"You don't expect me to believe that, do you?" she sneered "You must be dreaming." Tommy remained calm.

"Well you saw the mud didn't you? The soil around here is quite dark and somehow I had red mud on my slippers." Clarissa couldn't argue with that. She submitted herself to nodding resignedly.

"What about these footprints and the picnic?" she was desperate to disprove at least something that he had said.

"Not sure," came the answer.

"The person only came to me in the night, from the Kingdom, and I didn't know he could come and go as he pleased."

Clarissa was starting to get a headache.

"The Kingdom?" She asked. Tommy nodded.

"Tell you what," he said, suddenly having an idea. If she wanted to be involved in this, then why didn't he let her? She may well have an answer or two stuck in that pea-brain of hers. "Why don't you come with me tonight?"

"How do you know it will happen tonight?" Clarissa could feel a prickly sensation running up and down her back. She hadn't really believed Tommy to start with, she had suspicions true enough, but this seemed real. He wouldn't dare to invite her if this place and these people didn't exist, would he?

"I don't," Tommy said slowly. "If it doesn't then you know I'm a fibber. If it does, then you've got to help me sort all of this out."

"All of what?" Tommy couldn't believe his ears, wasn't she even listening to him?

"Well, it's not exactly normal is it? People appearing and doors appearing. Clocks that don't strike midnight and Kingdoms that exist between a grandfather clock and the fireplace." Clarissa nodded slowly.

"So this has never happened to you before then?" Tommy choked on his Coke.

"I don't think so," he snapped sarcastically. "What kind of a weirdo do you think I am?" They looked at each other for almost a minute in silence and then both burst out laughing.

"Sorry," gasped Clarissa. "I thought there was something strange about this house, but I never imagined it would be this strange. More to the point, why on earth did all of this start to happen as soon as you arrived?" Tommy shrugged his shoulders and at that moment David and Martha arrived at the doorway for more cold wine.

"What are you two up to?" asked David, immediately suspicious.

"Oh we were just talking about what happened today," said Clarissa flippantly. "I think it's time we went to bed now, right Tommy?" Tommy nodded sheepishly and followed Clarissa out of the door and up the stairs.

"Can I come?" whispered Clarissa.

"Be in my room before the clock strikes midnight," whispered back Tommy. Although it was only a little past nine, Tommy was relieved to be on his way to bed.

Chapter 13

Tommy lay very still. It had been quite some time since the clock had struck eleven thirty. Where was Clarissa? She had promised to come into his room as soon as the clock had struck the half hour. This was typical of girls, Tommy decided. They were always late for everything. Just as he was considering the situation, he heard voices coming up the stairs. It was Martha and his dad. His heart began to race, what if they saw Clarissa on the landing? They would know they were up to something and surely they would not approve. Certainly they wouldn't approve of the two of them conspiring in the middle of the night and most definitely not to attempt to travel back to The Kingdom. He listened with bated breath as footsteps came closer to his door and he snapped his eyes tight shut as he heard the door handle turn. Slowly the door opened a short way and he could see the light through his eyelids. He pretended to be asleep and tried his hardest to look peaceful and innocent.

"There," he heard his dad whisper. "I don't know why you worry so much. He's fast asleep already and probably dreaming up some rather inventive story about his own little world." There was a short pause and Martha replied, sighing as she whispered.

"Yes. I'm sure you're right. I just wish he could be at peace with us all. He has taken all the turmoil so hard."

"He will," came the response. "He just needs to take his time. Just look how much better he is with Clarissa even since Friday," he could almost feel them looking at

141

him. He could imagine them both peering around the door frame and being so happy together. No matter how hard he tried, he could not feel any resentment toward Martha. She did seem to be well intentioned and she really was trying to make him feel at home. He tried desperately to think about his mother, yet he somehow could not imagine her in an unhappy state. Since his father had left, she and Tommy had been happier. Tommy sighed without realising and Martha whispered.

"Let's leave him. He looks so peaceful." Slowly the door closed and the footsteps moved away toward their bedroom. Tommy started breathing again.

How long had they been there? Clarissa must have heard them otherwise she would already be here. It must be almost midnight by now, where was she? Surely she hadn't forgotten? If she wasn't here soon the clock would strike and she would miss Hoy-Paloy. How could he explain to Hoy-Paloy that someone else knew? Would she be able to see him? If she could, what would he say? Would he be offended? All of these questions were whirling in his head when suddenly the catch on the door clicked and Tommy drew a quick breath.

Slowly the handle turned and the door slid quietly open. There was Clarissa. He sat up and motioned to her to come over to his bed quickly.

"Where have you been?" he hissed. She pulled a face at him and quickly closed the door behind her.

"Quiet. Do you want them to hear us?"

He shook his head and waited for her to join him. She went around to the far side of the bed and knelt on the floor.

"I heard Mummy coming up the stairs so I couldn't come out of my room." She was dressed in a knee-length beige nightie and dressing gown covered in pictures of teddy bears and she wore slippers that matched. Tommy was amazed, he had never seen the like of them before. The moon appeared to be full at the window and lit the room quite well. Tommy could pick out the shape of each Teddy. He had thought that girls were supposed to mature more quickly than boys, but there had to be some mileage in those slippers.

"You'll get cold sitting there, come and sit in with me," Tommy whispered.

Clarissa drew back.

"I don't think so," she snapped.

"Oh shut up and get in, right now," whispered Tommy holding back the top of the covers, Clarissa did as she was told and together they sat and waited with bated breath, each wondering what would happen next.

Eventually the clock began to strike, neither of them had realised but they had both begun to doze. Leaning back against the large feather pillows, both had gently closed their eyes and begun to breathe quite deeply. Both of them sat up suddenly and stared around the room. There was nothing to see that had changed from before and Clarissa began to doubt that anything would happen. After what seemed like an age, the clock began to strike and they both counted to themselves, using fingers and nodding heads in order not to lose count.

'Ten, eleven...' they both counted and both waited and waited and still nothing happened. Clarissa eventually let out a big sigh that sounded quite irritated.

"Perhaps the clock is just broken?" she whispered and Tommy drew breath to defend himself but had no need.

"It most certainly is not broken my dear. I think we'd all be in quite some bother if the clock should somehow get broken." Clarissa grabbed Tommy's arm.

"Did you hear that?" she breathed. Tommy smiled.

Hoy-Paloy was here but where? Tommy could not see him anywhere in the room.

"Where are you Hoy-Paloy?" he whispered excitedly.

"Over here by the window young man." Both children snapped their heads in the direction of the window. Standing just below the window to the left, half-covered by the full-length curtain, was the small figure of Hoy-Paloy.

"What are you doing over there?" asked Tommy leaping out of bed and tripping over the edges of his pyjama trousers that were just a bit too long.

"I wanted to see what you had brought for me. I thought you might have tricked me." Tommy stopped short, mortally offended.

"Tricked you?"

"I can see quite clearly that is not so. I have to be so careful, you understand. I have to protect the others." Tommy quickly forgot to be too offended.

"What others? Can we meet them?" Hoy-Paloy nodded but held up his hand.

"Not so fast young man. I haven't been introduced. Where are your manners?" he inclined his head toward Clarissa who was still seated in the bed and stared in amazement, the bed covers drawn up to her chin. Tommy moved between them and gestured to each of them in a very solemn fashion.

"Hoy-Paloy, this is my step-sister Clarissa. Clarissa, this is my very good friend Hoy-Paloy." With that introduction Hoy-Paloy stepped forward and gave his deepest bow. His beard touched the floor and he almost toppled over in his sincerity. Clarissa whispered from under the covers.

"What's a Hoy-Paloy Tommy?" Tommy could have died from embarrassment. He looked from Clarissa to

Hoy-Paloy and back again. Hoy-Paloy regained his balance and snorted quite dramatically. The whole of his little rotund frame quivered with distaste.

"He's not a 'what', he's a 'who'," whispered Tommy sharply. Hoy-Paloy began to chuckle.

"At least we teach you some things Thomas Ravensdale," he whispered and bowed deeply to Tommy, who was quite taken aback by this and wasn't quite sure what to do next. Hoy-Paloy solved his quandary by standing upright quite quickly.

"Come, bring her if you must. We haven't got much time."

"Everyone keeps telling me that. What's the great hurry?"

Hoy-Paloy looked quite shocked.

"You still don't know?" he shook his head and scratched it so hard that he could feel waves of disapproval billowing from the direction of the bed. Clarissa had swung her legs over the side and keeping both eyes on the small creature before her, was reaching for her slippers. Securing both, she slid her feet into them and rejoined the conversation.

"It's The Something," she stated.

All three of them froze, as the moonlight from outside became obscured and a dark shadow fell across the window. Tommy and Clarissa both looked straight out of the window, but could see no reason for this sudden dimming of the light. Hoy-Paloy however reacted differently. He fell to his knees and covered his face with his beard and remained there, trembling for quite some time. Tommy went to him and crouched down to his level.

"What is it? Hoy-Paloy, are you hurt?" he took the small creature by the shoulders and shook him gently. Slowly Hoy-Paloy lowered his beard and a small, terrified face looked up at him.

"S… She must not name it. It grows stronger Tommy. We must go. We have less time and it grows stronger." Hoy-Paloy struggled to his feet and Tommy helped him as best he could. Turning to Clarissa he whispered sharply.

"Now look what you've done. Don't talk like that, it scares him." Clarissa was still looking out of the window. All the hairs were standing up at the back of her neck. There had to be a rational explanation for this. These sorts of things did not happen by themselves. Something was definitely not what it would seem here.

As she turned to follow the two boys out of the room, she was conscious that the light from the window changed again. Spinning round sharply she could see nothing different, but noticed that she could now clearly see the full moon again and the light from it streamed quite clearly into the bedroom. Shivering slightly, she hurried to catch the others before she was left behind. She had not been entirely convinced about what Tommy had told her and she had decided to come and disprove his ramblings. That was what she had convinced herself and yet now she was not quite so sure.

She followed them out onto the landing, sliding her slippers quietly to make sure that it would not be her that woke up Martha and David. The two of them seemed to know the routine. Hoy-Paloy reached for his key and slotted it easily into the keyhole. It was at the base of the panel of the long case clock and Clarissa had not noticed it before. Tommy beckoned to her and grabbed hold of her hand, she tried to pull away but Tommy had her hand firmly grasped in his. Stepping forward, the two of them broke into a little song, Clarissa did not know whether to laugh or cry. The way was quite scary and dark, yet the song seemed to make everything all right. Tommy had come back before, so it couldn't be that bad, could it?

"Hoy-Paloy is on his way.

He has a task to do this day.

Fliw the mystic made me this charm.

The purpose of which is to keep us from harm.

Pretty flowers and forests too.

Can we save them? Tommy, it's up to you."

Clarissa wished desperately that she had put on some other kind of clothing. She felt quite vulnerable in her dressing gown and slippers. They found themselves in Hoy-Paloy's cave once more and Tommy motioned to Clarissa that she should not pass comment on what she saw.

"Come, meet the others." Hoy-Paloy took Tommy by the hand. "Fliw is not here today, but the others want to meet you." Clarissa was entirely confused, who on earth was 'Fliw'? But she followed without question. She would have to remember these things for when they got back.

They emerged in Hoy-Paloy's cave, Tommy recognised it but Clarissa screwed up her nose in disgust.

"You wish to meet the others?" Hoy-Paloy asked Tommy, who nodded and wondered why he had not met them before. He opened his mouth to ask and Hoy-Paloy answered before he could speak.

"I had to be sure that you don't work for it. You could both come and spoil everything for us here." Hoy-Paloy turned his back to Tommy and began to search the horizon, through the open doorway.

"What is 'it'?" Tommy asked. Hoy-Paloy spun round and looked horrified.

"You know Tommy, the… erm… the S… the…"

"Something," announced Clarissa, suddenly arriving behind them. Suddenly everything changed. Hoy-Paloy fell to the floor again and clutched at Tommy's feet whimpering as he did so. The light changed to a dim green glow and it appeared that 'things' were muttering just out of sight. There were bushes and trees in this place and it felt as though they were in some kind of garden. There was short grass on the floor and the sky appeared to be a sort of blue-green. Tommy noticed that one of the suns had already set in the distance and only the rays of the one remaining shed it's light upon the world. In the distance Tommy could hear movement and all kinds of disapproving whispers.

Suddenly a voice rang out behind them and Clarissa jumped forward, grabbing hold of Tommy's arm.

"Talk of 'it', would you? I think you would change your mind if you ever were to meet it." Hoy-Paloy peeled himself from around Tommy's feet. Tommy was standing as if frozen to the spot. What on earth could be happening now? He was quite convinced that Clarissa would bring this whole world crumbling around their ears. Had she not heard the warnings he had given to her? He turned.

"What are you doing?" he hissed, shaking her free from his elbow. "You're going to get us killed at this rate you silly girl." Clarissa looked indignant.

"We can't be killed. This is just a dream. I can say whatever I want," she stamped her foot to emphasise her indignant attitude. Suddenly, the grass moved beneath her feet and she fell heavily to the floor.

"Ouch," she cried and sat rubbing her left elbow. "That hurt." Tommy looked wildly about, but he could see nothing untoward. Hoy-Paloy however stood upright and from behind a rock he pulled the most peculiar looking person either child had ever seen.

"What do you think you are doing, you mad fairy?" Hoy-Paloy shouted. "This boy is the 'one' and he has brought someone to help and all you can do is trip them up and make them feel thoroughly unwelcome." Tommy and Clarissa looked on in amazement. The creature Hoy-Paloy dragged out from behind the rock was indeed a fairy, but what a strange looking fairy she was. At about the same height as Hoy-Paloy, she was almost as broad around the middle as she was tall, and clad in the most pretty little pink ballerina outfit, with gossamer wings protruding from her shoulder blades. Hoy-Paloy dropped her at Tommy's feet in a crumpled heap.

"I am most terribly sorry Tommy," he said and bowed deeply. "We are a simple folk and Twinkle here was concerned for the young lady's disrespect of the... erm. You know." Tommy nodded.

"You can't say that word Clarissa. Otherwise we really will get hurt." Clarissa looked at him in a different light. Down here, these creatures seemed to respect him and talked as if he were something really special. She realised also, that even if this was a dream, Tommy believed that they could get hurt or even killed. She knew about the hurt bit and rubbed her elbow gently as they both studied the new creature that lay before them.

"Don't hate me Mr Tommy, please don't hate me. I thought I was doing my best for you," sobbed the fairy.

"I know who you are," said Clarissa suddenly. "You're the fairy who visited my great grandmother and left fairy dust behind." Tommy looked at Clarissa in amazement.

"What?" he asked. Clarissa dismissed this.

"Long story, I'll tell you when we get back. We've still got the fairy dust."

"Fairy dust?"

"Later," snapped Clarissa.

Tommy bent down and helped the fairy to her feet.

She was dressed in a small pink leotard which had a frill that later Clarissa told him was called a 'tutu'. On her feet she wore the most beautiful pink silk ballet shoes with ribbons that were laced all the way up to her knees. Her wings were almost transparent but hung limply behind her almost resting on her bottom, which stuck out at a most unfortunate angle. Tommy didn't really know what to say next. He looked at her wings.

"Those are the most amazing wings I think I have ever seen on a fairy," he said, hoping that he was not saying anything offensive to her. "Thank you for looking after me. I really do appreciate it. Clarissa here didn't know what she was saying." Clarissa snorted and stepped back, she was no longer the centre of attention and this really did not impress her. Twinkle however was won over immediately and blushed slightly as he spoke. Her wings slowly unfolded themselves and began to swing back and forth. Tommy noticed that she had a small wand in her hand and he looked at it and smiled. It was around six inches long and had a small pink metallic paper star stuck on the end. The star was most crumpled and looked as though it would fall off if touched. Twinkle looked at it in dismay.

"Hoy-Paloy, just look what you've done to my wand you fool," she squeaked. Hoy-Paloy took the wand from her and flattened it out as best he could. He then returned it to Twinkle.

"You should be more careful with it Twinkle," he said in a most serious manner. Twinkle shrugged and turned her back on them all. As they watched, her wings began to flutter and she slowly raised her round little frame onto the points of her toes. There appeared to be a lot of effort involved and suddenly Clarissa spoke.

"Gosh, that's really clever. I never got that far at

ballet lessons you, know." Tommy smiled at her. She seemed to have come to terms with their situation. This helped Twinkle, who turned on her points and looked squarely at Clarissa.

"You mustn't talk about 'it' you know. We never do, but 'its' moving on its own now." Hoy-Paloy stepped forward.

"You be quiet, you hear, you stupid fairy. You're just as bad and he won't like it you know." Twinkle fell silent but pirouetted slowly for the children. Tommy marvelled at how such tiny points could keep aloft such a robust frame. Then he decided that those wings were most definitely working harder than they looked.

Suddenly Twinkle lost her footing, or maybe her concentration and wobbled.

"Oh, do be careful," Tommy said before he could stop himself, but too late – she was falling. Falling was a graceful word for what happened. The small round figure of the fairy wobbled first one way and then the other and then finally capsized in a pink and shaky heap. As she hit the ground a small puff of coloured sparkling dust shot or rather spurted from the end of her wand. Clarissa rushed forward to help. Hoy-Paloy put his head in his hands, but Tommy watched the patch of ground on which the dust had fallen. Slowly a little shoot came pushing through the short grass and a small purple pansy unfolded its petals and moved around toward the light.

"Are you OK?" asked Clarissa as she helped Twinkle to her feet. Twinkle looked as though she was about to cry. Clarissa desperately tried to think of something to cheer her. "I do like those shoes, they're so dainty and pretty." Twinkle perked up immediately.

"Oh do you?" she gasped. "I do like to make an effort you know, but it doesn't always pay off to my advantage."

Clarissa tried to hide her amusement, this small ungainly creature meant her no harm and she obviously really needed some help with her dress sense. This was exactly the sort of thing she was good at, thank goodness they'd got here in time.

Tommy was still looking at the pansy. Hoy-Paloy joined him and they both inspected the flower.

"She does mean well you know," whispered Hoy-Paloy. "She just can't quite get it right." Tommy smiled and pointed at the flower.

"Does she always do that?" Hoy-Paloy nodded.

"She tries so hard with her magic, but she really hasn't got it together. Fortunately that is one of the nice side-effects. She also has a plot for a dieting spell whereby she doesn't have to stop eating chocolate biscuits to lose weight. As you can see, that one hasn't quite worked either." Tommy grinned. She certainly hadn't got that one sorted. Hoy-Paloy continued. "You have to give her credit though, she will not give up trying." Twinkle had regained her confidence somewhat with Clarissa's help.

"Do you like my flower Tommy?" she asked. Tommy could not hide his feelings.

"It's the most beautiful flower I've ever seen grow so quickly," he replied. Twinkle almost stumbled in her delight. Then she tried to balance back on her points again. It took quite some effort, but slowly she raised herself again, her wings working double quick time in an effort to keep her aloft.

"I can do flowers on purpose," she said and waved her wand along the ground. Sparks flew and fairy-dust spurted sporadically from the tip of her wand. True enough, a bank of pretty flowers began to grow along the side of the path they were walking upon. Hoy-Paloy cringed again.

"Don't encourage her Tommy, please. She'll get all

big headed and then anything could happen." At this point Twinkle stumbled and fell again, she landed with an unceremonious thud at Tommy's feet. He and Clarissa both bent down to help her.

"Go away," she gasped. "I don't need your help. I'm Twinkle the fairy. I'm going to keep you safe whilst you are here in The Kingdom." Hoy-Paloy rushed forward and dragged her to her feet.

"Don't you be disrespectful now, you foolish fairy. These children are trying to help you, so they are." Tommy and Clarissa smiled to themselves and continued walking whilst Twinkle regained her dignity.

Chapter 14

Slowly Tommy became aware of a noise in the distance. It sounded like some sort of engine and it was getting louder as he listened. He turned to Clarissa.

"Can you hear that?" he asked. Clarissa nodded and they stood frozen to the spot whilst the noise became louder and louder. The ground began to shake and they felt as though the noise would surely explode their eardrums, when Hoy-Paloy suddenly shouted.

"Casey. It's Casey Smokestack. Look! Behind you Tommy, at last the others are coming to meet you." Tommy turned to face the direction in which Hoy-Paloy was pointing. What he saw made him gasp and reach for Clarissa's hand. There across the grass, and steadily chewing up the flowers Twinkle had just created, was a huge old fashioned steam train. It was the kind of train that had a cattle guard on the front of the engine and just had to be from the Wild West. This could not be. What kind of world had they entered? Tommy and Clarissa stood transfixed by the apparition before them. The train bore down on them at a terrifying speed and it felt as if it would surely run them down and kill them all. Yet right at the last minute the engine veered slightly to the left and swerved most unnervingly.

The pistons controlling the wheels screamed with the tension of braking from high speed and the whole vehicle shuddered to a halt less that a few metres in front of them. Tommy breathed a sigh of relief and let go of Clarissa's hand. Clarissa could not move from the spot. She could not believe that the engine so recently bearing down upon them could have stopped so incredibly close to them. She was surely going to give the driver a serious piece of her mind. A huge plume of smoke issued forth from the splayed smokestack of the engine and the whole vehicle hissed with heat from the strain of such immense effort. Hoy-Paloy dashed to the side of the engine and looked up onto the foot plate.

As they watched in amazement, Tommy and Clarissa gasped as the driver of the train emerged through a screen of smoke.

"Howdy all," came a very old American drawl and slowly the owner of the voice came into view. Casey Smokestack as Hoy-Paloy had called him was every bit as corny as his name suggested. Clarissa couldn't help smiling at the vision that met them.

He must have been at least six feet in height and wore a pair of old grease-stained denim dungarees. On his head he wore an old pin-striped cap of some seersucker material that matched his western-style shirt and around his neck was a red and white spotted handkerchief. On his feet he wore old fashioned leather boots and in his hand he carried a pair of leather gauntlets.

"Casey," shouted Hoy-Paloy. "Come and meet him."

"Him?" asked Twinkle, most confused. Hoy-Paloy ignored her and continued.

"He is the one. Come, we must help him as quickly as we can." Casey nodded and leapt down from the engine and crushed even more of Twinkle's pretty flowers.

"Oh do be careful," shouted Clarissa. "Twinkle tried ever so hard to make those flowers." Twinkle slid over to where Clarissa stood and took hold of her hand. Even though she had thought that Clarissa had been stuck up when she first met her she was now beginning to like this child of the humans. She seemed to understand what it was like for Twinkle and how hard everything was for her. Maybe she would help her to be noticed by Tommy. After all Tommy was the one and she, Twinkle, had an opportunity to be noticed by him.

Tommy on the other hand was inspecting the engine. He could not believe how large the machine was. He had learned about the Wild West at school and about how pivotal the railway had been in terms of securing many places, but he had not realised just how powerful these engines really were. He studied the cattle fender on the front, the size of the smokestack and how it belched the most foul smoke he had ever seen into the air. Then there was the foot-plate and small holes in the metal where the driver had looked out to see where he was going along the track. The track – Tommy suddenly realised there had been no track. The engine had slewed along the ground and had chewed up most of Twinkle's flowers finally grinding to a halt not far from where they stood.

"Hey Casey," he shouted. The driver came trotting over to them and stuck out a hand for Tommy to shake. After shaking his hand, Tommy asked. "How does this work?" he pointed at the floor and the engine, which was sinking steadily into the grass next to where they stood. Casey grinned and spat a lug of tobacco on to the ground.

"Well, I don't rightly know youngster," he said, in his slow American drawl. Clarissa screwed up her nose in disgust. That had to be the most disgusting thing she had ever seen in her life, until Casey then pulled down his sleeve and wiped the spittle from his mouth along the seam. She could contain herself no longer.

"Mr Casey," she snapped. "That has to be far and away the most disgusting thing I have ever seen in my whole life. Where are your manners?" Casey, Tommy,

Hoy-Paloy and Twinkle all stood and looked at her dumb-struck. She continued quite unabashed at the silence that greeted her. "You arrive here without so much as a by your leave and you trample all of Twinkle's pretty little flowers with your dirty great big engine. Then you spit all manner of filth onto the grass. I don't know who you think you are, you are most certainly not the sort of person we wish to consort with. Am I right?" There followed very long silences, Hoy-Paloy looked back and forth between Tommy and Clarissa and his mouth opened and closed several times. Eventually Tommy took charge of the situation.

"Clarissa," he said sharply, and everyone turned to look at her. "Shut up." There was a deathly hush and then he continued. "I haven't brought you here to criticise these people. I brought you here partly because I thought you could help and partly because I thought you might like to be involved. Please don't fall out with the good guys. I'm sure there are plenty of bad guys you can fall out with. Right Hoy-Paloy?" Hoy-Paloy nodded, his eyes shone. These were the sort of qualities he had hoped Tommy would have, yet he hadn't expected to see them quite so soon.

"Let's all make friends Tommy," he said and his eyes looked to Clarissa as though he were laughing inside. Solemnly they all shook hands with each other and introduced themselves. Casey then became quite concerned.

"I'd better go put the engine away before she digs up the whole flower bed." With that he leapt back onto the engine and they watched it slowly pull backwards and away to a firmer piece of ground. Clarissa and Tommy both marvelled at how it moved without sinking into the soil. Tommy turned to Clarissa.

"Do you have to embarrass me in front of these people?" Clarissa looked at the floor. She was sure she wasn't cut out for this kind of adventure. She hadn't realised it was going to be quite so dirty and unpleasant.

Twinkle sidled up to her and slid her chubby little hand into Clarissa's

"Don't worry," she whispered. "You're still my friend, even if the boys are mean and horrid." Clarissa found comfort in these words, yet she wondered how low she must feel to take sympathy from an obese and failed fairy. She took a deep breath as Casey trotted back up to them again.

"Right," said Hoy-Paloy. Suddenly he took charge. "Only one more introduction to go tonight. Where can he be?" Clarissa took all of this in.

"Tommy?" she enquired.

"Yes?" he responded, noting the earnest tone of her voice.

"Why are we meeting people like this?" Tommy shrugged and looked at Hoy-Paloy. Hoy-Paloy smiled sheepishly and wiggled his head from one side to the other.

"If we are to help you, then we need to introduce ourselves."

"Help us?" Clarissa didn't like the sound of that. Casey turned round and spat on the floor again, wiping his mouth on his other sleeve. Realising what he had done, he suddenly snatched off his hat and held it by the rim.

"I'm sorry ma'am," he said sheepishly. "I'm not as civilised as you folks, but if you'll be forgivin' me for my indiscretions, we needs your help, we do. We needs you to help us fight the… The… We just needs you, that's all." Clarissa could feel the hair on the back of her neck standing up all by itself.

"You mean The Something, don't you?" she asked quietly. Twinkle snatched her hand from Clarissa's and dropped in a little heap to the floor, sobbing and holding her head. Casey looked as though he had been struck dumb and Hoy-Paloy stopped dead in his tracks.

"Clarissa." This from Hoy-Paloy. "We may be simple folk, but please don't mention that..." suddenly they all became aware that the light was dimming. So much so that it was hard to see each other. The temperature suddenly dropped and Clarissa clutched her dressing gown around her. They all stood in perfect silence and held their breath for what seemed like an age. Slowly, the light became normal and the temperature returned to an acceptable level.

"Hoy-Paloy," whispered Clarissa in a very small voice, "what was that? Was that the...?" Hoy-Paloy nodded and she had no need to finish her question. They all stood quite still for a few moments. All except for Twinkle, who continued to sob miserably into her tutu. Clarissa dropped to her knees.

"Twinkle. Please don't do that, it isn't that bad. It's not as if 'it' can hear us," she looked up for reassurance, but none came. Hoy-Paloy stood slowly nodding his head and she felt a wave of near panic pass over her. She corrected herself. "It's not as if 'it' heard us," she stroked Twinkle's back and gently rubbed between her wings.

"I don't know so much..." Casey whispered gently. "But we seem to have got away with it this time," he looked about him, chewing all the time and spat a big glob of 'baccy' as he called it, right over one of Twinkle's best flowers. Clarissa snorted, that really was too much. She pulled Twinkle to her feet and dusted off her tutu.

"Well Tommy," she said in a most business-like fashion. "What exactly do you propose we do next?" They all looked at Tommy as though they expected him to say something. Tommy was, however, still contemplating the magnitude of a sixty tonne engine that ran on no tracks and he failed to answer.

They all stood waiting for Tommy to speak, slowly he realised that the silence had gone on for too long.

"What?" he asked, looking quite bemused from one to the other. "Have I missed something?"

"Only just," replied Hoy-Paloy.

"What?"

"Oh, never mind. What do we do next?" asked Clarissa. She was becoming impatient and if she was going to be set upon by a strange being whilst wearing her dressing gown, she needed to get on with it right this very minute.

"What's that?" Casey asked and instantly spat more 'baccy' which landed on Hoy-Paloy's shoe. Hoy-Paloy gave him the most awful stare and went to wipe it off on a tuft of grass.

"What's what?" Clarissa again took hold of Twinkle's hand. Twinkle shuffled close to Clarissa and buried her head in Clarissa's dressing gown. Her wings drooped and her wand bent ever so slightly downwards. In the very distance they could all hear a sort of buzz, a static kind of hum. No, it was as if an electric tram were just about to swing into view.

"Look," shouted Tommy to Hoy-Paloy. "Over there." Hoy-Paloy nodded and they all turned to face the direction in which Tommy pointed.

Slowly, over the dim horizon, an object came into view. It was quite small and distinct and hovering some six to eight inches above the ground.

"Oh no," groaned Twinkle. "Not him." Hoy-Paloy nodded and they all waited expectantly whilst the craft approached. It was a small craft just big enough for one passenger. It appeared to be a 'teardrop' shape, with the tapered end pointing forward. In colour it was bright red and the side carried a long stripe of silvery white along its length. The whole craft was tapered into a smooth rounded entity and Tommy gasped as it drew nearer.

"What? What is it?" whispered Clarissa. She was struggling to hold onto anything tangible right now and she needed something concrete on which to focus.

"It's Brett, Brett Trailblazer." Tommy turned to Hoy-Paloy. "What on earth is he doing here?" Hoy-Paloy nodded slowly.

"We do try to keep up with the other side you know," he said, nodding more strongly now. "He hasn't quite become used to his purpose here yet. He still requires careful scrutiny, but his intentions are good."

"What? What are you talking about? I need to know! I demand to know!" Clarissa stamped her teddy bear slippers on the grass. Disappointed at the lack of sound she continued. "Do you know this thing?" she lifted the hand she still held with Twinkle. Twinkle stood resolutely by her side and stuck out her chin mirroring the indignance that Clarissa obviously felt. Tommy turned to look at her he was surprised by this outburst.

"You wanted to come, remember? You said earlier that you wanted me to prove to you that all of this was real. You didn't believe me. Now you can jolly well be quiet whilst we meet the bravest and most handsome star fighter in the universe." Twinkle groaned and Clarissa turned to her.

"Do you know this Brett?" Twinkle nodded.

"He is a real show off and he thinks that all the ladies adore him. He doesn't even come close to Tommy." Clarissa thought about this as the small craft came ever closer.

"Tommy? You really think that he's wonderful?"

Twinkle nodded. "You're so lucky. You know him 'outside' and he speaks to you. I don't know him, yet. I intend to. He is the most wonderful person ever, but I wouldn't dare to tell him. I'd just make a fool of myself in front of him. You saw what I did when you first came here." Clarissa nodded and held Twinkle's hand tighter. What a poor unfortunate creature. How could anyone be besotted with Tommy? She turned and looked at him as he waited for the craft to land and she saw him in a slightly different light. Here was a small puny boy that she had been determined to hate and despise for the whole of eternity. Yet he had brought her into an adventure she was not sure she had the constitution to finish.

As the craft approached Tommy, they could all hear a low electronic hum. It seemed to fill the air and Twinkle hid again behind Clarissa to protect herself from whatever was about to land.

Tommy stepped toward the craft. He could not believe his eyes. This was a replica of the craft that he always chose on his computer back at home. The pilot of the craft was called Brett and Tommy was curious to see who or what would step down. Suddenly the craft landed with a jerk on the grass, amongst Twinkle's most pretty flowers,

"I'm going to have to say something to whoever, or whatever is flying that thing," whispered Clarissa. "Just look what they've done to your prettiest flowers." Twinkle doubted it very much. Clarissa hadn't met Brett yet and she didn't think that a rebuke or admonishment were anywhere close to what would happen next.

Clarissa stepped forward and pushed Tommy out of the way. Hoy-Paloy looked most annoyed, but Tommy just smiled and brushed his blond curls out of his eyes. The top of the craft hissed as steam and pressure vented from the release of the door. As the top flew up Clarissa was forced backward by the power of it and fell heavily on her behind.

A tall and distinguished looking figure stood up from the front of the craft and stepped out into the view of the assembled friends. The figure had on a red lycra suit with white lightning flashes down the front and back. He had on red boots to match and a red helmet that was not dissimilar to a motorcycle one.

He leapt out of the craft and pulled off his helmet. He must have been at least six feet three inches tall. He made the rest of the small band of friends feel very small indeed. As he pulled off his helmet they all noticed how his short blond hair stood on end. The cut was almost military in style and the stance he took was as if he were 'on a mission'. The man leapt down from the craft and went straight to Clarissa who lay, still dazed from the shock on the grass. Clarissa looked up at him and felt her knees turn to jelly. As he looked down at her she felt as if she never wanted this moment to end. As she looked over the whole of his body, she could see the muscles rippling through his suit. She vowed that she would never settle for any of the puny wimps that were to be at the pony club dance. Brett was definitely her hero.

Kneeling down, Brett picked up her hand and kissed it gently.

"How can you ever forgive me? I apologise from the bottom of my heart. I could not foresee this tragedy and I hope you will forgive me," he gently placed her hand back down and Clarissa wished desperately that she had put on some other clothing. How embarrassing could it be to meet the man of your dreams wearing your childish nightie and matching dressing gown?

"Brett?" Tommy enquired, to which Brett stood back from Clarissa and perched his helmet under his arm.

"Yes Sir," shouted Brett, saluting with his right hand.

"What are you doing here?" he enquired, not quite sure that he needed to know the answer.

"I came to help you," replied Brett, as though that was the most normal thing in the world.

"How can you help?" asked Clarissa, standing up and brushing herself down. Brett shook his head slowly.

"You have no idea who I am and you have no idea who you are up against, do you?" Clarissa stood for a while and contemplated this.

"You are right. I have no idea who you are," she stated quite clearly. Tommy could not let this go by.

"Brett is the bravest and most accomplished flier in the history of 'Zero Gravity Grand Prix.'" He announced triumphantly.

"What?" asked Clarissa.

"A commuter game," whispered Twinkle.

"You mean computer game," corrected Clarissa. Twinkle again hid her face. Clarissa immediately felt guilty and gave Twinkle a hug. Twinkle soon forgot her sadness as she had found a friend. "Well, what's he doing here exactly?" she continued. Tommy turned to Hoy-Paloy for this one, but Hoy-Paloy shrugged his shoulders.

"We try to keep up with you Tommy, but you don't make it easy. Brett is the most recent addition to our team. He is as you said quite correctly from the computer game 'Zero Gravity Grand Prix'."

"Forgive me. I mean no harm to my trusted friends." Brett stepped forward and shook Tommy firmly by the hand. They stood for a while and contemplated each other. Eventually Tommy turned to Hoy-Paloy.

"Who else are we to meet. You said we are to meet people who will help us? Or rather that we will help the people that we meet." Hoy-Paloy took a step backward.

"Tommy, you have heard how you are to help us. You have met 'him' only yesterday and you know what you have to do." Tommy wasn't sure he liked the answer.

"But where is 'he' then?"

"You do not need to meet him today. You have come to meet the rest of the team," he turned and looked at 'the team'.

There was Clarissa, who looked as though she could quite easily faint at Brett's feet. Then there was Brett, who swanked around as if he was going to save the universe entirely on his own. Standing next to him was Casey, who was quite unsure of himself and between each spit of 'baccy' was intermittently apologising to Clarissa for his bad manners. Twinkle – now Twinkle was the only one who had proven her 'skills' and that appeared so far to be the ability to create pansies out of nothing, although it was true that skill was only as proven as the amount of times they had seen the pansies thrive. Twice was Tommy's most recent thought, but then he quite realistically expected it to become more before the adventure was completed.

Standing next to him at a full one metre, or so he had claimed, was Hoy-Paloy. Tommy thought that there was more to him than met the eye. Although he had not yet proved it, Tommy believed that Hoy-Paloy was not just a little goblin and was determined to prove otherwise. Tommy felt quite small. All of these strange characters were waiting on him to provide them with the answer, but he couldn't even begin to contemplate what the question might be.

Soon they all wandered to a shady patch of grass

under a large willow-type tree and sat down to discuss what to do next. Clarissa sat next to Brett and Twinkle sat right next to her, but also where she could hear every word that Tommy uttered. Hoy-Paloy sat next to Tommy and Casey sat furthest down the bank, desperately trying not to place any more tobacco in his mouth. Tommy spoke next. He might as well be honest with these people.

"You are all good people," he began. They all nodded fervently. "I want to help you as much as I can. I don't quite feel up to the magnitude of my task…" Clarissa interrupted.

"Oh give me a break." Twinkle hid her face in her tutu with shame, how could anyone even dare to interrupt Tommy? "You know why you're here, you told me earlier today. You're here to save all these people and this land from The Something. We're all supposedly here to help you." There followed quite a long pause. Twinkle slid over to Tommy and grabbed hold of his pyjama jacket, hiding her face behind his rib cage. She could feel everything falling apart, what on earth was going to happen next?

Chapter 15

As they sat under the tree, they could all see the sky cloud over and felt a cold, chilling breeze sneak upon them from the direction of the cave. As the light dimmed, Casey spoke in a low whisper.

"Beggin' your pardon Ma'am, but ain't you s'posed not to mention the... erm? 'Cos if'n you does, then bad things'll happen to us all." They sat still and contemplated the wisdom in these words. Twinkle piped up next.

"You know you're not supposed to. Hoy-Paloy told you. Like he's told me over and over." Hoy-Paloy was quite touched by this; he had always thought that Twinkle had never listened to the long talks they had together, yet it would appear that she had. The temperature continued to drop and a small cloud developed on the horizon and came towards them. They all drew away from the entity that appeared before them. Twinkle began to sob quietly.

"It's here. What shall we do? We're doomed," she buried her face in Tommy's pyjamas. He instinctively put his arm around her and tried to comfort her.

"It's all right Twinkle. You leave this to me. I've got this sorted," he took a breath. Hoy-Paloy was impressed. He hadn't been sure when he had brought Tommy to this world, but here he was taking charge and not doing a bad job at that.

"So what exactly are you going to do Tommy?" asked Clarissa. She looked cynical as the entity swiftly approached them. Tommy faltered slightly, but Twinkle came to his rescue.

"He's going to save us," she whispered. "No one can stop him. He's our hero," her belief was complete and Tommy couldn't let her down, not now. For some reason he stood up and faced the entity alone. Clarissa sat dumbstruck by what she saw.

"What do you want?" he challenged. "We are no threat to you today. You have no purpose here. Be gone." They sat and waited with bated breath and slowly the entity moved away and eventually dissipated over the horizon.

"My Hero," cried Twinkle. She grabbed hold of him and hid her face in his pale blue pyjamas. The rest of the company had to agree with this. They all nodded in appreciation as Tommy turned and regained his seat under the tree.

Presently Hoy-Paloy spoke.

"That is enough for today. It's time we took you back." Clarissa looked at Brett, who had instinctively moved to protect her from the on-coming threat and had effectively thrown himself over her body. She now struggled to her feet and could feel herself go a very unflattering shade of puce.

"Tommy," she began, trying to feign some sort of authority. "Is it time we were leaving? We have to get on with our other work." Tommy looked at her in amazement. What other work? He could not think of anything more important than where they were right now. As the second sun slipped slowly and gracefully over the horizon, it bathed them all in a deep reddish-purple glow. He could not think of anywhere else that he would rather be at that precise time. Hoy-Paloy intuitively sensed the unease and intervened.

"Maybe we should go back through the gateway Tommy?" he stood with his back to Clarissa and winked knowingly, raising his eyes toward the darkening sky. Tommy nodded and the three of them set off toward Hoy-Paloy's cave.

Clarissa knew that the other two were not speaking to her and she kept her own counsel. They climbed up the hill through the undergrowth and entered Hoy-Paloy's home. As they moved toward the gateway she stopped.

"I am sorry, you know," she said to Hoy-Paloy. "I didn't mean to offend anyone." Tommy turned his back and wished he had not brought her to this place. Soon they reappeared in Tommy's bedroom and Clarissa quickly said her goodbyes and returned to her own room.

Meanwhile back in The Kingdom, Twinkle had returned to Fliw's home.

"Help yourself to a cake Twinkle," said Fliw, although he was aware that she had already reached for the tin on the top shelf of his larder. 'Those wings,' he thought, as he imagined her hovering in a most ungainly fashion several centimetres from the stone floor of his kitchen. "You may bring us both a mug of hot chocolate if you wish." Twinkle didn't need to be invited twice, she made herself busy with the kettle. She had filled it with water from the well and was placing it gently upon the stove when suddenly.

"Who is it? Who's there? You are not welcome here. Be gone you foul witch." Fliw was shouting at someone outside the door. He sounded very angry. Twinkle gasped, she hoped he wasn't angry with her.

Using her wings very quietly, she lifted herself onto the very end of her toes and half-flew, half walked across the kitchen to the door. She peeked timidly around the edge of the door, which was almost closed. Sure enough, there was Fliw standing in the middle of the room with his arms outstretched and he was shouting in the direction of the front door. Fear engulfed her and she dared not enter the room, so she stayed hidden by the door and hoped that no one would notice her. Fliw spoke again.

"Be gone, foul demon, you have no place here." A harsh cackle followed from outside the door.

"You are weak, old man. You have lost your powers. The 'one' has returned to the other side and you are left alone to face your enemies." Twinkle stopped breathing, she could not believe her ears. As she held her breath, her wings stopped moving and she fell heavily to the floor with a thud. She lay still, very still and hoped that she would not be found.

Fortunately for Twinkle, at the exact moment that she fell the wooden front door shattered into thousands of shards of flame. Smoke billowed into the room and everything went black. Twinkle hid her face with her arms and lay sobbing gently into the cold quarry tiles of the kitchen floor, her whole body quivering from head to toe.

Eventually everything began to settle and the noise died down. After a while Twinkle lifted her head and surveyed the rubble that had once been the dwelling of Fliw the Hermit. The kitchen was mostly untouched. She was lying under a gentle layer of black dust and she soon shook it out of her wings and brushed most of it from her hair. The front room however was a completely different story. As she gingerly crept around the kitchen door small heaps of door splinters smouldered gently all over the space that had been a most elegant front room.

Suddenly there was a piercing whistle and Twinkle stumbled to the ground again, trembling with terror at what new misfortune had now surfaced. It was obvious that Fliw was no longer here and that she must face this new threat alone. After what seemed like an eternity to Twinkle, the kettle began to boil dry and the whistle turned into a gurgle and eventually into a desperate wheeze. Twinkle plucked up enough courage to return to the kitchen and remove the dry kettle and turn out the light on the stove. She stood, wings folded and laden with black dust, and surveyed her predicament. In the absence of Fliw, the next most important person to tell was Hoy-Paloy.

Meanwhile Hoy-Paloy left Tommy and Clarissa in the fireplace in Tommy's bedroom and returned to his home. As he materialised at the end of his roughly hewn bed he looked quickly around him. Something did not feel right. The hairs on the side of his face stood on end and bristled in the static that filled the air. There was no immediate evidence of anything untoward, yet still the bristles in his beard twitched as if by themselves. Moving to the entrance of his abode, he noticed that although the two suns were not yet set the sky appeared to be a darker hue than normal. A sudden pang of fear struck his heart, so powerful that it almost physically hurt. The Something, it had to be The Something. Where was Fliw?

He hurried down the bank, through the undergrowth and trotted along the pathway that led to the cottage at the side of the lake. He burst in through the hole that had once been the front door without a care for courtesy or even the respect of a warning knock. The building was empty. A fire still smouldered in the hearth, yet no one was at home. Confused and with a mild panic showing on his face, Hoy-Paloy returned to his home to think about what to do next.

What had happened to Fliw was that he was having a really bad time. He stood with his arms outstretched and defied the demon at his front door. He prayed that Twinkle had the sense, or was scared enough not to show herself to his torturer, Schwartzkopf the witch. She was an agent of The Something and she would not settle until he was destroyed. He hoped beyond hope that Twinkle would be able to summon help. What help would he need? In truth he needed Tommy, but how would he get to him? The only way was through the gatekeeper, Hoy-Paloy. He had served him well these last few centuries and he needed him now. If only he could be certain that the fairy would summon him…

Suddenly the door exploded in front of him and there stood Schwartzkopf. It was exactly what Fliw had dreaded. He knew his powers were weak and he knew that she would come on the order of her master. How he wished he had been stronger or that Tommy had been more confident. Either way his power was depleted and he was now at the mercy of this repulsive creature.

"Will you not invite me into your home Hermit?" Schwartzkopf stood in the doorway and sneered at Fliw. He shook his head.

"If you enter my home it is without my invite," he responded. The witch laughed at this and stepped eagerly through the doorway. Once inside, she paraded around the room and looked down upon Fliw, who struggled with the intensity of her stare.

"You will come and be held by him," she snapped. Fliw stood his ground and responded.

"No. You will take me against my will," she snorted in response. "However," and dismissed it with a wave of her black clad arm.

Somehow, Fliw was taken. If he had been asked, he would have been unable to tell how. He moved as if in a daze and he could not escape from the direction of travel. He followed Schwartzkopf, her aura something to behold. She was very distinctive and had an evil presence about her. Fliw knew her of old: she was an agent of The Something. She would never exist without it and he was sure that The Something would be much the weaker without her.

She swept out of the building with a flourish and Fliw could do nothing but follow in her wake. She had no physical contact with his body, yet somehow he could not do anything but her bidding. Fliw tried to resist, he slowed his feet and tried to stop, but he could not. One foot went steadily in front of the other and soon they were at the end of his path. Now clearly resisting, Fliw began to struggle and turn his feet back toward his house. He turned his head and he was sure he caught a glimpse of pink fairy peering from within. He tried with all his might to contact Twinkle telepathically, but Schwartzkopf sensed this and flew into a rage.

"You will stop that right this minute," she screamed and cast a binding spell on his mind. Fliw could not even remember why he was resisting. To him everything was complicated. He knew he was not happy to go, but he could no longer remember the reason for this. Head bowed, he turned and submissively followed Schwartzkopf away from the safety of his home and away from Twinkle and Hoy-Paloy.

Twinkle had almost caught his telepathic message and she pressed both hands to the sides of her head in an attempt to think clearly. This was not easy for her and she frantically ran out to the front of the house to make eye contact with Fliw as he disappeared. She was too late. As she came out of the house she could just about make out the two figures as they disappeared around the bend in the lane. What should she do? What had she ever got right, ever that is? Twinkle was not renowned for having good ideas. Neither for being able to sort out problems when they arose. Sadly she sat at the end of Fliw's path, all thoughts of cake had now vanished. How she wished that

Hoy-Paloy were here to help her. Hoy-Paloy! Of course, that was what Fliw was trying to tell her, wasn't it? She must go and tell Hoy-Paloy, he would know what to do. She stood up suddenly and dashed off in the direction of the cave. It never occurred to her that she should see which direction they were heading towards. In her haste she fled up the trail to the cave.

Fliw followed the witch reluctantly along the path. He had no idea where they were headed, but he had a pretty good idea who or rather what was at the end of the trail. Desperately he tried to make sense of the fog that filled his head, but it was no use: he was truly under the enchantment of this vile creature. The witch muttered incantations to herself as she led him along and made sure that she did not waver from her task. She would not dare to fail as the consequences would be unimaginable.

Eventually, Fliw lifted his head to see where they were. He could no longer remember why he was reluctant to travel this way, but he knew that there was something wrong. Something? That was a familiar word, even through the spell: he weighed the word in his mind. It felt like a bad word, yet he had no concept of how or why this was so. As they travelled, they had passed through trees and bushes and as they emerged from the undergrowth a trail wound its way to the top of a hill in the distance.

Chapter 16

At the top of the hill stood a castle built of the darkest stone Fliw had ever seen. The structure was immense and must have been large enough to house many thousands of men. A whole city could have been housed within the smooth and sinister walls. From the bottom of the slope, Fliw had to crane his neck to see the top of the building. It stood so high on the hill that wisps of cloud could be seen winding around the many spires at the tips of the towers. Towers the like of which Fliw had never seen before, or had he? The sight stirred something in the darkest recess of his mind. Desperately he struggled with the partial memory. It appeared to Fliw that the whole building was smouldering gently as if in preparation to burst into flames at any time. He did not recognise this place, nor could he remember how they had arrived there.

The witch turned to Fliw and with a flick of her hand commanded him to stop. He stopped in his tracks and surveyed her slowly, desperate to recognise something about this creature, if nothing else the most repulsive form with short, bent limbs. In appearance she could be described as painful to the eye. Fliw knew he could not trust her although in his current predicament he could do nothing about her.

Meanwhile Twinkle was making great haste toward Hoy-Paloy's cave. To say that she was running would have been a misstatement. True enough, her little chubby legs were moving as quickly as she could make them, and her wings were beating as fast as she could physically flap them without them bumping together.

"Must tell Hoy-Paloy. Hoy-Paloy, must get to Hoy-Paloy." As she scrambled through the undergrowth toward the cave, strange things she had not seen before began to move on either side. Determined to get help, she ignored them and pushed on through the foliage. As she tired, she was convinced that the leaves and branches were trying to hold her back. It felt as though brambles were deliberately becoming caught on her tutu and several small rips appeared as she forced her way through. A small furry creature suddenly brushed against her and she squealed falling to the ground. It had gone very dark where she lay and the whole of the little thicket seemed to move and grow around her as she trembled, nursing scratched legs and arms. Panic engulfed her and she cried for help.

"Hoy-Paloy, Brett, Casey. Is there anybody there? Help me. Help," she cried.

"Hoy-Paloy, Brett, Casey…" A small voice echoed right next to her. She snapped her head around to see what had spoken. There came a mocking laugh and then. "Help. Who will help Twinkle the fat fairy? All alone in the thicket." The voice was right next to her left ear and she twirled her head, but not quick enough. Twinkle began to cry softly, she was all alone and scared.

Suddenly there was a crashing noise behind her and Twinkle curled into a tiny ball. Hopefully whatever this new demon was would not see her and perhaps leave her in peace. A familiar voice rang out loud and clear.

"Make way. Coming through. Be gone, foul pests. Out of the way, don't you dare get in the way of Brett Trailblazer on a mission to save poor Twinkle." Twinkle uncurled quickly and as she stood up Brett came lumbering through the undergrowth.

"Brett, Brett," she cried, the tears still wet on her

cheeks. She threw her arms around the top of his leg and clung to him. Brett looked down in amazement.

"Twinkle, what is it? What's wrong?" he tried to peel her arms from around his leg but she clung even tighter to him. All that he could get from her was.

"Hoy-Paloy, must tell Hoy-Paloy." And that was all he could make out.

It was in a most peculiar fashion that they emerged from the thicket. Brett with his sleek profile, clad in his lycra racing suit and Twinkle still clutching his left thigh and now with her legs wrapped around his ankle. Slowly, he hobbled up the bank and opened the heavy door to Hoy-Paloy's cave.

"Hello?" he enquired in his booming tone. "Are you there little man?" As they stepped inside, the light from the fireplace glowed in a friendly fashion. Brett suddenly realised how dark the sky had become outside. He quickly moved inside the dwelling and closed the door with a resounding thud.

As they waited patiently, Hoy-Paloy slowly materialised close to the hearth and jumped visibly as he became aware of Brett and Twinkle.

"What? What's happened?" As his eyes became accustomed to the darkness, he saw Brett with Twinkle wrapped around his left leg in a very sorry state indeed. Brett looked most uncomfortable and his stained and pulled uniform showed how dire their journey to his home had been.

"Found her in a bit of a spin," reported Brett, becoming quite military in his approach. "Can't think what had happened to her. The thicket was closing in and some of the wildlife were taking advantage." Twinkle at this point dropped to the floor and heaved a massive sigh. Brett reached down and picked her up into his arms.

177

"Don't have a go at her, though. We need to know exactly what happened, these scratches didn't just happen by themselves little man."

Hoy-Paloy looked at Twinkle. She was obviously upset, but she never, ever had appeared to him with mud stains, tear stains and scratched arms and legs before. Not to mention the blackened wings she had that were now hanging limply behind her. This was definitely not the Twinkle he had come to know and love over the years and this most definitely required explanation.

"Put her in the best chair," gestured Hoy-Paloy. Brett did this, although the best chair in Hoy-Paloy's home was not much more than a wooden base with slim cushions. Twinkle curled up again and sat with her knees tucked under her chin. Brett felt most awkward, he had never quite mastered this sympathetic stuff with girls. Girls were most certainly an enigma to him. The two boys moved towards her and then sat on the floor looking at her.

"Would you like a drink?" asked Hoy-Paloy, not sure entirely what he would give to her. Thankfully she shook her head. Taking a deep breath she began to speak.

"We have to get him back," she said quite firmly.

"Who?" asked Hoy-Paloy, thinking immediately of Tommy.

"Fliw, of course," she retorted. "Where's Tommy? We need him as well." Hoy-Paloy and Brett looked at each other and a certain element of brotherly bonding took place.

"Why?" asked Brett, picking thorns out of his shiny red outfit.

"Because we are all going to be in very big trouble if we don't." Twinkle nodded her head to emphasise this point. "We have got to sort something out right now. Otherwise The Something will win."

At this the whole room fell silent and all three of them looked at each other hoping that someone else would speak first. None of them did and the moment turned into an age. Brett spoke next.

"Start at the beginning Twinkle, and then we'll be able to help." Twinkle took hold of Brett's suit and shook him as hard as she could. How could they not understand what she was saying? Soon she resigned herself to do their bidding.

"Right." She took a deep breath. "I would like a drink of hot chocolate." Hoy-Paloy dashed to his stove and put the kettle over the hot plate. Twinkle enjoyed this rather, as it was usually her who had to carry out these tasks and she enjoyed the attention. Brett crouched over Twinkle.

"So, little fairy," he began, "tell us your tale." Twinkle looked from Brett to Hoy-Paloy and decided she had their attention.

"Well," she began, "when I was at the house of Fliw, Hoy-Paloy had taken Tommy home." Brett looked at Hoy-Paloy and nodded. Twinkle went on. "I went to make tea in the kitchen and a most horrid thing took place." Both of the boys nodded in encouragement. "Suddenly, Fliw was talking to someone outside the door and he was quite cross." Brett and Hoy-Paloy exchanged glances. Twinkle continued. "The front door exploded and there she was."

Suddenly there was a crashing blow to the door of Hoy-Paloy's residence. Twinkle grabbed hold of Brett's leg again and hid her face from the door. Hoy-Paloy went to the door and opened it cautiously, then threw it wide open.

"Come in friend," he said. The relief in his voice was obvious. Twinkle peered around Brett's leg and to her immense relief there stood Casey. When he saw Twinkle he let out a sigh of relief.

"There you are," he said. "I heard you calling and couldn't find you, so I came to get some help. What happened?" Brett interrupted.

"We were just about to find out," he said, gesturing to Twinkle who was still firmly attached to his leg.

Casey came in and Hoy-Paloy closed the door behind him.

"There's a fair old storm a'brewin out there," he drawled in his deep American accent. "The sky's gone almost to black it has." Again, Brett and Hoy-Paloy looked quickly at each other. Brett picked Twinkle up and sat her on the edge of the dining table where they could all see her clearly.

"Come on Twinkle," he said encouragingly. "Tell us what happened." Twinkle looked from one to the other and gulped deeply. The edges of her wings were still trembling as she began her tale again.

"I was with Fliw and we were going to have tea." They all nodded reassuringly. "Then someone came to the door and Fliw didn't want them to come into the house." Again they nodded. "Then the door exploded."

"Exploded?" enquired Casey. Twinkle nodded.

"Yes. There was black smoke and flames and sparks." Twinkle waved her arms over her head to emphasise the enormity of the occurrence.

"Who was it?" asked Hoy-Paloy, but he thought he knew the answer before it came.

"Her. It was her... the witch that works for... The... works for it." Twinkle did not dare say the name of either the witch, Schwartzkopf or of The Something. She did not want to bring any more trouble on her or her friends. All three of the friends stood back and looked at each other.

"What happened then little fairy?" asked Brett, not sure that he wanted to hear any more.

"She took him."

"Where?" Hoy-Paloy was pulling on a jacket. They could all hear the wind buffeting the front door. There was most certainly a storm on its way.

"Don't know. I came to get help. She took him without touching him." Casey was puzzled.

"You mean he went on purpose?"

Hoy-Paloy shook his head slowly.

"No. She must have put a spell on him." Twinkle nodded, she could see Schwartzkopf waving her arm at Fliw in her mind and she shuddered. Her wings flapped slowly and then hung limply behind her.

"Don't worry little fairy," Brett boomed in his most sympathetic manner. "You did exactly the right thing and we're going to save him. Aren't we chaps?" Twinkle looked a little more hopeful at this suggestion and looked back to Hoy-Paloy. Hoy-Paloy, however, did not look quite as enthusiastic as he fastened up his jacket.

"It's raining now," said Casey. True enough they could hear the rain pelting against the front door. Soon it was hammering and the wind was howling relentlessly. "What do we do next?" he went on. Hoy-Paloy turned and faced them all.

"We have no idea where she has taken him but we do know what she has taken him to." All four of them nodded solemnly at this. "In order to get him back we have first to find out where he is and how he is being held. Then we can form a plan to get him released."

"How will we do all of that?" Twinkle asked in a very small voice. She was not much in favour of going outside in the wind and rain, it sounded very wet and very cold.

They all looked at each other for what seemed like ages. Suddenly Twinkle sat bolt upright.

"I know," she announced triumphantly. They waited

with bated breath. "We need Tommy. He'll save us." There was a sudden silence and even the wind seemed to quieten for a few moments. Twinkle sighed and sank back down again. She wished she could just once come up with a good idea that everyone liked. Slowly Hoy-Paloy began to nod his head.

"Yes. You're absolutely right Twinkle. We need Tommy to help us. Fliw brought him here and said that he was the one who will save our world. I must go and find him," he turned toward the fireplace and contemplated his next move.

"He's already been here today though hasn't he?" Brett asked. "Can he come back again? How will you contact him?" Hoy-Paloy shook his head.

"I have absolutely no idea. But we can't leave Fliw to the devices of those two, can we?" On this they all agreed and it was decided that Hoy-Paloy should go and find Tommy as soon as possible. Hoy-Paloy removed the two golden keys from the invisible casket and placed them around his neck. He stepped toward the fireplace, inserted the big golden key into the lock and disappeared.

Chapter 17

Meanwhile, Tommy had arrived back in his bedroom quite tired from the excitement of developing his druid skills with Fliw and Hoy-Paloy. He had coped well with Clarissa who had left The Kingdom in some sort of temper. He wondered if it wasn't just all too tiring to worry about. He took off his slippers and climbed into bed. Within a few minutes he was sound asleep, but he was subconsciously restless. He dreamed about Fliw and The Something. There was a storm, the wind was howling and the rain was lashing down. He did not recognise the place he was in and he made a conscious effort to stop this dream but to no avail.

In his dream, Tommy was walking in the rain. He had no coat or hat and his feet were bare. The road on which he walked was muddy and he could feel the coolness of the rainwater between his toes. As he looked down, he realised that he was wearing his pyjamas and that he was already soaked to the skin. Looking up he could see in the distance a hill upon which sat a castle. He could not remember ever seeing it before and he did not recognise the landscape. He was filled with a feeling of deep foreboding and he was quite relieved when he suddenly woke.

As he lay still in his bed, Tommy could hear the wind outside his window and the rain lashing against the glass. He considered how strange this was, when he had climbed into bed the weather had been quite calm. He lay and worried a little about his dream and puzzled over how vivid and realistic it had been. After a while he began to doze again and he wasn't quite sure whether he was awake or dreaming when the quilt on his bed began to move.

The corner of his quilt was tugging quite definitely to his left and he opened his eyes slowly. He found himself face to face with a very worried-looking Hoy-Paloy. He jumped and sat up quickly.

"What on earth are you doing here?" he whispered. He could tell there was something wrong. "Why have you got a coat on Hoy-Paloy?"

Hoy-Paloy took a deep breath.

"Tommy," he began. "We need your help. You have to come and help us now."

"Now? But it isn't twelve o'clock now. How will we get there and back?" Hoy-Paloy nodded.

"I know, but I can't leave Fliw on his own with the witch. She has bewitched him and taken him to The Something. His powers are weakened and he is vulnerable. You have to help, even Twinkle is involved. We are all threatened this time and you are the only one who can save us." Tommy slid out of bed and stuck his feet into his slippers. Then he took them off again.

"On second thoughts, I think the weather is bad on your side. I need to put something else on to combat the storm." Hoy-Paloy's eyes widened.

"How did you know there was a storm?"

"Well, is there?" Tommy suddenly thought of his dream; there had been a storm and outside the weather was not good. He had just assumed, or had he? He was not sure. Hoy-Paloy nodded.

"It is not a natural storm." Tommy raised his eyebrows and Hoy-Paloy continued. "It is caused by The… by The Something. It is all things evil and only the one can save us all." Tommy shook this thought off and padded softly in bare feet to the wardrobe. He took out his wellington boots and a raincoat. Putting them both on, he turned back to Hoy-Paloy.

"Well gatekeeper. What do we do now?" Hoy-Paloy stood quite still for a moment and then approached Tommy. He had more confidence in this boy's inherent ability now than he had ever done. Yet somehow there was more he felt that they could do.

"What about her?" he asked quietly and looking at the floor in order that Tommy would not think that he was challenging him. Tommy was not sure who he meant. "Her who upset Twinkle." Then he knew, it was Clarissa.

"Good thinking," said Tommy. For some reason, this was a huge relief to Tommy. At least he was no longer alone with his dream world and he could ask for help, although he was not certain how receptive she would be to this idea at some unreasonable hour of the night, especially after what she had just been through. "You wait here, Hoy-Paloy. I'll go and get her." Hoy-Paloy nodded and went to stand by the window. As the door closed quietly behind Tommy, he began to pace up and down the room. He had never been quite so agitated, all of his world was at stake here and he suddenly realised how much Casey, Brett and even Twinkle really meant to him. They all had their own little character traits, yet he loved them all in his own way. He was most apprehensive and did not realise that he had paced back and forth so consistently until Tommy's return.

Meanwhile back in the other world the three friends looked at the spot where Hoy-Paloy had vanished.

"D'yall understand this stuff?" asked Casey. "'Cos it's all a bit beyond simple folks like me." The other two looked at him and smiled sympathetically.

"Some things just are," said Brett, nodding wisely and

wishing to goodness that he understood even half of what had happened in the last few hours. He was just glad that he had been there for the little fairy. He had quite a soft spot for her and had been most distressed when he had heard her cry for help. Although just lately he had felt a little peculiar when 'Her' had come from Tommy's world. She was possibly the most interesting thing he had ever met.

"What are we going to do now?" asked Twinkle.

"How do you mean?" asked Brett.

"Well, we're here and we don't know how long Hoy-Paloy will be and Fliw is somewhere else and something awful is bound to be happening to him." All three of them nodded in agreement, yet none of them came up with an answer.

Tommy quietly opened his bedroom door and sneaked along the landing. This was not easy in a heavy raincoat and wellington boots, yet he was determined to succeed. He carefully opened the door to Clarissa's bedroom and shut it quietly behind him.

"Clarissa?" he whispered. "Are you awake?"

"I am now," came a husky response. "What on earth do you want at this time of night?" she sat up and pressed the light on her alarm clock. It was exactly one thirty in the morning. "Oh goodness! Tommy, what do you want now?" If Tommy had been on any other mission he would have admitted defeat and retreated to his own room. This time however, he was determined to carry it through.

"Something awful has happened," Tommy hissed. "Put some warm clothes on. Hoy-Paloy, Casey, Twinkle and Brett need our help. Just do it. Do it now."

Clarissa sat bolt upright.

"Brett?" she asked. "Brett needs my help? I must come right now." Tommy's eyes lifted to the ceiling. This was embarrassing, she was only a girl and he was he most accomplished anti-gravity race driver in the history of the world. She didn't stand a chance. Hold on. What was he thinking? This was absurd, although everything he had encountered since he had been at this house had been absurd.

"Clarissa, just put something warm on, there's a storm in The Kingdom. You need a coat and some wellington boots and something to fight off a witch." Clarissa needed no further bidding, she leapt out of bed and put on a tee shirt, some sweat pants, her riding boots and a Barbour waxed jacket. Tommy lifted his eyes to the ceiling again; she couldn't just wear a coat, it had to be a designer label. Even though the whole world as they knew it was in danger, Clarissa had to be appropriately dressed. He sighed.

"What?" enquired Clarissa.

"Nothing," muttered Tommy. Then she picked up her riding crop and flicked it once or twice.

"What are you doing?" whispered Tommy,

"If I need to fight, then I need to be armed," she said quite succinctly. "If Brett is in trouble then I need to protect him with whatever means I have available to me." Tommy could not argue with this, although he could not quite see how a small riding crop would influence Schwartzkopf the witch. He was however a little perturbed that she had been so totally enthusiastic to return to their world, but because Brett was in trouble she apparently needed no encouragement.

They both sneaked back toward Tommy's bedroom were Hoy-Paloy was most agitated. Tommy opened the door and was met with,

"Where have you been? There isn't much time you know." He nodded and all three of them immediately left the bedroom again and approached the grandfather clock. Hoy-Paloy used his key and they entered as if it were midnight.

"I thought this only worked at midnight," whispered Clarissa.

"So did I," responded Tommy, not quite sure if they were on a course to nowhere. A quick look at the face of the clock had told him it was just a little past two in the morning and he prayed that everything would work just the same.

As they travelled through the gateway into the cave, they began to recite their rhyme.

"Hoy-Paloy is on his way.

He has a task to do this day.

Fliw the mystic made me this charm.

The purpose of which is to keep us from harm.

Pretty flowers and forests too.

Can we save them? Tommy, it's up to you."

Strangely, none of them felt reassured by this and as they sang it they all felt most insecure. As they traversed the cave they could sense other things moving in the outer edges of their environment. Hoy-Paloy's voice was thin and wavery and they were not quite sure that he had this under control. They could all sense 'things' just beyond their vision and the feeling came to a head.

"Hoy-Paloy?" It was Tommy who spoke,

"Yes?" he responded.

"What is happening?" Hoy-Paloy shook his head.

"I cannot say. We need your help more than ever we did. You must save us from what lies ahead."

Tommy took Clarissa's hand. He could sense a feeling of fear and he knew that he was not entirely happy with events as they were occurring. Without any prompt from himself Hoy-Paloy fell back and took Tommy's hand. It was in this way that all three of them passed into The Kingdom. Tommy, Clarissa and Hoy-Paloy all entered Hoy-Paloy's cave hand in hand. As they arrived, Tommy was most apprehensive about what they would encounter.

Chapter 18

The sight that met them was more or less the sight that Hoy-Paloy had left. In his front room were Twinkle, still brandishing the scars of her encounter, Casey not entirely sure of anything, and Brett who was desperately attempting to make sense of why he was here.

"Hey," began Brett, "you're back, and thank goodness who you've brought with you." Clarissa went straight over to Twinkle and put her arm around her.

"Oh no," she began, "What has happened?" Twinkle sniffed and whispered.

"Schwartzkopf has taken Fliw and the storm outside is really, really bad. I don't know what we will do." Clarissa saw the scratches on Twinkle and appreciated the trauma she had been through.

"Where has she taken him?" she asked, Twinkle shrugged her shoulders.

"Don't know." Clarissa sighed and looked around.

"We're going to see where the trail leads to," said Brett. Clarissa immediately responded.

"Where from Brett?" She was infatuated with him and was desperate to show that he had the situation under control.

"Twinkle said that Schwartzkopf took Fliw from his house. There has to be a trail, they cannot have disappeared into thin air and we intend to find out where they went. You, dear lady, must look after the little fairy whilst we're gone and ensure that no harm becomes her." Half of Clarissa wanted to dispute this command and yet somehow the other half desperately needed to do his bidding. Eventually Clarissa nodded and sat down next to where Twinkle still sat on the edge of the dining table.

"Let's go then," said Hoy-Paloy and the four friends looked at each other for reassurance. Hoy-Paloy opened the front door and they disappeared into the night. Once the door was closed, Clarissa set about making hot chocolate for her and for Twinkle.

"So," she asked, "tell me everything that has happened since we were last here." Twinkle puffed herself up and began to tell Clarissa the whole story.

Meanwhile the four boys went out into the storm. The undergrowth had taken on a life of its own and they struggled down the side of the hill. Tommy had to ask some questions.

"What is happening here?" he asked. Casey answered him.

"There's foul things afoot here abouts Tommy. Don't you go thinkin' you can tackle them on your lonesome." Tommy considered Casey's words as they descended through thick foliage and pouring rain he was quite inclined to agree with him. As they continued their journey, Hoy-Paloy started to speak.

"Oh, we know that she took Fliw against his will and we know she took him away from his home. So if we go to Fliw's house and try to retrace their steps then we should have a pretty good idea which direction they took!" Brett continued in his dramatic tone.

"We'll get him back and take him home to the lovely ladies." Tommy looked at him. He was almost as sad as Clarissa, they were definitely both the saddest cases Tommy had ever seen, although it had to be said that their intentions were honourable. Hoy-Paloy looked over his shoulder at Tommy and raised his eyes to the sky. The sky was most definitely the darkest grey Tommy had ever seen. The clouds were most threatening and the rain pelted down on them without mercy.

"I think we should go back for them," Tommy said suddenly. Brett nodded and Hoy-Paloy retraced his steps as the others waited. Within minutes he returned with the 'ladies' in tow.

"They wouldn't be left any way," Hoy-Paloy started. "They were coming out of the door as I got there." Clarissa flashed a look at Tommy and he didn't even want to begin to reproach her.

They continued on their way, heads bent into the wind and shoulders bowed against the ferocity of the storm. Soon they arrived at Fliw's house. The door was missing and the interior was a complete mess. Brett and Casey stepped inside to investigate. They had not expected to find anything and they were not surprised with the results of their investigations. Hoy-Paloy seemed to lose some hope as he stood at the gate.

"What do we do now?" he asked forlornly as he and Tommy waited patiently. Tommy surveyed the scene, the rain pelted down as he looked up and down the lane. Suddenly he saw a familiar route: he was looking at the trail from his dream. The trail was where he had been walking in his pyjamas. He stared at the path before him and took hold of Hoy-Paloy's hand. Hoy-Paloy shouted to the others and they set off on their way.

Tommy felt most uncomfortable, this felt as though he was reliving something that had happened before. He continued and they walked for a good while before they turned a corner and surveyed what Tommy had dreamt about. Before them on the top of the hill stood the castle and in this light it was more menacing than Tommy had remembered.

"This is where he is," said Tommy. All of them stood and took in the sight before them. In the half-light the castle was even more imposing than Tommy had dreamed it and the spires above the structure seemed almost alight with fire or fumes of some kind.

"So what do we do now?" asked Casey. He was the most uncertain of all of them and just wished that the adventure was over.

"I have no idea," replied Tommy. "All I know is that we have to breach the walls and rescue Fliw the hermit." They all stood and acknowledged this statement for a while. Presently Hoy-Paloy spoke.

"We have to move soon," he said and they all nodded in agreement, yet somehow not one of them wanted to move first. Tommy closed his eyes and imagined. He could feel the presence of Fliw and he could also feel the presence of The Something. This was a feeling he had no way of conveying to the others and he made no mention of it to them.

"Let's go," Tommy said and he led the way forward toward the huge structure before them. The path was running with water and they trailed through deep mud on their way toward the castle. Strangely Tommy thought about the mud he had carried back the first time to the house and he noticed how this was the same reddish colour. It was of no consequence however, as this time he had to continue with his journey.

As the companions approached the main entrance to the building they were dwarfed by its enormity. They stood at the moat of deep murky water before a huge raised drawbridge and lowered portcullis and all looked across the moat on the wrong side of where they stood.

"What do we do now?" asked Casey, somewhat disheartened by what he saw.

"We find a way in," replied Brett in true heroic style. Tommy took a deep breath and nodded. Hoy-Paloy looked up at him quizzically and Tommy shrugged his shoulders.

"So how do we do that?" Hoy-Paloy was beginning to lose hope.

"Don't know, but we can't let Fliw deal with this by himself. Not in his weakened state."

Hoy-Paloy nodded and stood back, waiting for Tommy to do something, although he was not quite sure what.

Tommy took in a very deep breath and all five of the others looked at him in amazement. As Tommy concentrated, he began to lift slowly from the ground. Another deep breath as he willed himself slowly higher until he had some two metres of clearance from the ground where they stood. The wind and rain seemed to subside a little as he lifted and they all willed him to move forward. As he moved Tommy looked carefully around him. If he was to land on the other side of the moat he would need to propel himself forward a good twenty metres to the other side. He was not entirely convinced he would be able to do this by himself.

He remembered the words of Fliw that he must not deviate from his purpose, concentration was the key to this task. As he concentrated, he spoke in a broken English.

"Need your help," he said hoarsely. Hoy-Paloy was the only one who heard and Tommy wasn't sure that he had contacted him verbally. It felt just like he had contacted him telepathically as he had heard it called, but he tried to maintain his concentration. He dropped slightly as he wondered if Hoy-Paloy could read his thoughts. This alerted the others and they gasped as he suddenly dropped lower.

"Concentrate Tommy. Don't be distracted," shouted

Hoy-Paloy and Tommy rose back to his original height. Hoy-Paloy seemed to know what Tommy needed and he turned to the others. "We must help him," he cried. "We have to help him to levitate over the moat to the other side."

"How?" wailed Clarissa, and Tommy sighed as she slapped her hands and the riding crop against the sides of her waxed jacket.

"Quick, hold hands," Hoy-Paloy shouted "we have to 'think' him over to the other side." Clarissa opened her mouth to question this further, but Twinkle shoved her and she stumbled into Brett.

Brett grabbed hold of her hand.

"Come. We must help," he boomed and snatched up Twinkle's small chubby hand in his free one. Then Brett, Twinkle, Clarissa, Casey and Hoy-Paloy all held hands and took a deep breath. Not one of them dared to breathe either in or out until Tommy was safely over the moat and determined that he should now lower to a small platform just outside the raised drawbridge. This drawbridge appeared quite solid from the other side of the moat, yet from where Tommy now found himself there was a gap of more than a metre between it and the portcullis.

Tommy felt quite tired from his efforts, but he was determined not to let Fliw down. He was entirely consumed with the challenge that awaited him. Quickly surveying the drawbridge he called once more upon his newly learned skills. He stuck his head through the lattice of the portcullis and identified the workings of the winding mechanism to the drawbridge. He focused his mind and willed the mechanism to turn and as he did so he half wondered how a stronghold such as this could be left unguarded. It should be obvious to all that he at least would be attempting to rescue Fliw.

"What are you doing?" called Clarissa. Tommy could be so infuriating. He had dragged her out of bed in the middle of the night and expected her to follow him through some horrendous terrain. All of this to rescue an old man for some bizarre world that believed him to be some sort of saviour. Twinkle gasped and put her hand over her mouth. Clarissa turned to face the fairy. What was even more bizarre was that such a feeble creature would venture out into a horrendous night and follow him to the ends of eternity. This worried Clarissa and she contemplated that maybe it was only she who thought that this was a wasted journey. After all, the only reason she had consented to come here at all was Brett. She looked at him now and suddenly realised that he was looking right back at her.

"What?" she asked. Brett shook his head briefly and turned back toward Tommy.

Tommy appeared to be accomplishing something at least. He stood with his head inclined at a peculiar angle and with his hands clasped around the posts of the portcullis. As the company watched through the sound of the wind and rain that now had turned into a downpour, they could hear the creak of the drawbridge winding mechanism. As it slowly lowered to the ground they peered at the other side of the moat. They stood transfixed as the huge wooden bridge slowly came to rest with a resounding thud before them. Brett suddenly sprang into action.

"Quick," he yelled. "Let's get out of sight before anyone sees us." Without looking back he sprinted across the wooden platform and toward Tommy. The others automatically followed and they soon found themselves at the foot of the dropped portcullis. Tommy seemed distracted but he motioned for them to come to him.

Clarissa went up to him and whispered.

"What on earth are you doing?" He looked back at her passively.

"I am here to save Fliw. What are you here for?" In the honesty of the moment, Clarissa could not give away her true reason for getting there but nodded in acceptance of their purpose. They all looked up at the portcullis and Casey said, "We can get through that easily."

"How?" asked Hoy-Paloy, who was still struggling with the enormity of what had been executed by such a novice. Casey approached the structure and ran his fingers slowly over the joints in the rustic struts. The struts were bound crosswise with a string twine. This twine seemed to be of some sort of thread and Casey concluded that this should be combustible.

"I think," he began hesitantly, "that this twine is crafted from flax and if that is the case, then it will burn with ease." All of those assembled on the small platform looked at each other.

"Casey," asked Hoy-Paloy, "how do we set it alight in these conditions?" They all agreed that the weather was most inclement and it appeared that this notion was to be found a failure. Casey, however, produced a tinderbox from the pocket at the front of his dungarees and his face relaxed; at last, he would make a positive contribution to proceedings. He turned his back on the company and hunched his shoulders against the wind. As they watched he opened his small tin and produced both tinder stone and flint that he placed carefully out of reach of the weather. With this equipment he carefully struck a spark that was not extinguished by the turmoil of the weather and he slowly lit the twine that held together the struts of the portcullis.

This was the most resourceful of plans and even

Tommy was humbled by the experience, so much so that he stepped forward and patted Casey on the shoulder in encouragement. Soon the twine was spent and the structure hung in a forlorn manner from the walls of the castle. It was most unnerving that no one seemed to know or care that six determined travellers wished to gain entry to the castle.

Presently they stood, huddled against the wind, on the very front doorstep of the immense structure. Not one of them appeared to feel the need to make the first move. Hoy-Paloy was on the outermost edge of the company and his feet were most definitely the coldest.

"Shouldn't we do something?" he enquired, hopping gently from one foot to the other and they all nodded consent, yet somehow still nothing happened. Then Clarissa spoke.

"Good Grief. I haven't come from my bed at some ridiculous hour of the night to stand on the front porch of this evil threat to mankind until I reach my twenty-first birthday. Will someone please decide what we do next?" Brett nodded with enthusiasm.

"Well said," he announced. "Tommy, it's up to you." The entire company turned to face Tommy and he desperately searched for appropriate words.

"Well," he began, to which Clarissa rolled her eyes to the tempestuous sky, "we have to find Fliw and rescue him." Everyone nodded at this and waited expectantly for more. Tommy was in uncharted territory now. "Hoy-Paloy, do you know this place?" Hoy-Paloy hopped again from one foot to the other and shook his head miserably. Tommy looked at the rest of the company. "Where would you keep a prisoner like Fliw?" There was a silence apart from the howling wind and driving rain. Clarissa snorted.

"Where would you normally keep a prisoner in a

castle like this?" she slapped her riding crop against the top of her boot with impatience. Twinkle moved around the group driven by a strange curiosity. She wondered what purpose that stick would serve. It looked quite severe, yet somehow she was sure that Clarissa would not use it against any one of them. Maybe she intended to use it against Schwartzkopf and The Something. Following another few more seconds of silence Clarissa sighed with a great deal of sarcasm.

"Well, I know I'd keep a prisoner in the dungeon." More slapping of the crop against her boot. "Am I the only one keeping up with this story?" There was another pause and Hoy-Paloy looked at Tommy.

"Right," announced Tommy, "that's decided then, we look for the dungeon. In my experience dungeons are always downstairs in the cellar," he said authoritatively.

"How many dungeons have you had in your experience?" asked Clarissa, most annoyed that Tommy again appeared to be making himself the centre of attention. The rest of the company turned their back to her and clustered around Tommy. It appeared that he was in control of this situation and they were desperate for a lead. Clarissa snorted and reluctantly joined the rest of the party.

"What do you want me to do Boss?" enquired Casey. Tommy looked at the solid and dependable chap.

"You stay here on guard Casey, I need someone to keep this passageway clear." Clarissa raised her eyes to the ever-petulant sky.

Brett moved close to her and quietly asked, "Do you not believe in our leader sweet lady?" Clarissa was so taken with this question that she forgot all about Tommy's arrogance. She nodded meekly and responded.

"He's so inexperienced I worry that The Something

will take advantage of him and us all." Brett gasped.

"You should not name it, that will be our downfall," he grabbed Clarissa and looked deeply into her eyes, Clarissa was so overcome that she nodded meekly and submitted to what ever was decided next.

Chapter 19

Tommy decided that they should all stick together and find the dungeon. Once they had found what means were restraining Fliw they could develop a plan to extract him.

"This way," said Hoy-Paloy quietly. "There's a passageway and some stairs going downward." They all moved quickly toward the steps and Tommy, of course, counted all thirty-two of them as they descended. At the bottom of the stairs, the passageway widened into a corridor with large closed doors on either side. The corridor was built of the same dark stone as the outer walls of the castle and was dimly lit by burning stakes bracketed to the walls. Each of them hesitated as they looked down the unpleasant passage.

"Come on we can't stop now." Tommy led the way and he grabbed one of the torches from its bracket as he passed. This inspired the remainder of the company and they followed close behind.

"How will we know which one is Fliw's?" whispered Clarissa. Hoy-Paloy shot her a reproachful glance. He was expecting more obstructive comments from her. She fell silent and they walked onward.

"This one, it's this one," proclaimed Brett as they passed by a door that stood slightly ajar.

"But it's not locked," said Twinkle, who had been very quiet for the most part of their journey. She really wasn't happy in dark places and being underground wasn't at the top of her favourite things list. Brett bent down in order to whisper to her.

"He may be locked inside a spell," he whispered into her ear so that the others couldn't hear. Twinkle did not like this thought and wailed.

"If he's locked in a spell cast by Schwartzkopf, we've got no chance of setting him free." The others looked at her uncertainly. The thought had most definitely occurred to Hoy-Paloy but he had thought it better to keep it to himself for the time being.

"Quiet you silly fairy," he snapped and Twinkle cowered behind Bretts' legs. Tommy spoke next.

"Don't tell her off Hoy-Paloy. I think she's very brave to have come this far, in fact I think we all are. Let's not argue we need to stick together." Hoy-Paloy nodded and Twinkle felt very proud and a little embarrassed that Tommy had spoken up for her.

Tommy crept toward the slightly open door and peered into the gloom within the room beyond. Brett stood right behind him ready to help at the slightest hint of trouble. Tommy turned, however.

"I have to do this alone now. You stay here. I'll be back as soon as I can." The others watched proudly and a little apprehensively as Tommy disappeared quietly into the room.

Inside the room, Tommy held the torch above his head in an attempt to see further. As his eyes adjusted to the dark, he could just make out the shape of Fliw standing in the centre of the room.

"Don't come any closer boy," he was not certain whether he had heard the words spoken or if they had been in his head. But it was definitely Fliw's voice and he responded.

"I've come to save you Fliw. How can I save you if I can't get to you?"

"You must will me free Tommy. I cannot move, I am

bound by an enchantment and it may have traps set around the edges." Tommy stood and contemplated this for a while. It was most disconcerting, he could see Fliw and he could almost touch him if he reached out, but he could sense that there was some force between them. He thought silently for a while and presently a little voice said behind him.

"Tommy, are you hurt? What is happening? Do you need us?" Twinkle had appeared at his side and peered past to see what Tommy was looking at. She saw Fliw and ran to him. "Fliw, Fliw, you're all right." As she came close to Fliw, there was a brilliant flash and poor Twinkle fell to the floor stunned and shocked, but thankfully unhurt.

"Twinkle, be careful," whispered Tommy. "You have to be patient. Tell the others what you have seen and let me try to free him." Twinkle struggled to her feet and limped sadly back to the door.

"Schwartzkopf will know that someone is here and will come to investigate soon. Tommy, you must hurry. It will not be long before The Something returns." The voice in his head had become quite urgent in tone and Tommy nodded that he had understood.

Lowering the torch slightly he made eye contact with Fliw and slowly tried to will away the spell. He could feel that it was working slowly but it was taking a great deal of concentration and effort. A small knot of fear suddenly developed in the pit of Tommy's stomach yet there visibly appeared to be no reason for this. Fliw broke eye contact with him and glanced into the corner of the room behind the door.

"Concentrate boy," said the voice. "Don't fail me now." Tommy was desperate to turn and look at what new threat had appeared but he heeded the warning and continued to battle the force.

Outside the room, the friends waited hardly daring to breathe, when suddenly from behind the door came the most hideous cackle that sent shivers down their spines and set their hair on end. Schwartzkopf. Where had she come from? She certainly hadn't come past any of them, they had stood quite still where Tommy had left them. They grabbed each other and waited with bated breath for whatever would happen next.

Schwartzkopf hovered around the room chanting and pointing at Tommy. The words she uttered were strange and mystical, her arms turned in great circles but Tommy continued with his task. He could feel the barrier around Fliw weakening. This spurred him on to concentrate harder. Schwartzkopf hurled a ball of fire at Tommy, quickly followed by a second and third.

Tommy froze for a second and then raised his left hand to block the oncoming danger. The fire was soon extinguished as the barrier around Fliw weakened even more.

Suddenly he felt the force give and Fliw began to move. His left arm flew out from his side and there was an enormous clap of thunder. Tommy continued to concentrate on Fliw, mostly because he was too terrified to turn and face the witch, but he knew he could not give up now. There was a brilliant flash of coloured light and a strangled gurgle from behind him. He could no longer resist the temptation and he turned to see what had happened. Behind him, all that remained of Schwartzkopf the witch was a small blue puff of smoke and as he watched it dissipate before his eyes, Tommy stood and stared at the place where the smoke had been and his mouth fell open.

Meanwhile Fliw's powers were sadly depleted and he

sank slowly to his knees. The exertion of extinguishing the witch had taken its toll and he could feel consciousness slipping away from him. Relieved that Tommy had turned his back Fliw took several deep breaths and tried to regain his composure. Tommy turned around again just as Fliw returned to his feet, clasping his staff for support.

"Are you hurt Fliw?" he asked, rushing forward to help. The hermit shook his head slowly and regained his composure.

"Where are the others?" he asked. Tommy turned and dashed to the door, flinging it wider the remainder of the company burst in all shouting at once.

"What happened?"

"Where is the witch?"

"Are you two OK?" asked Twinkle bringing up the rear.

"Is everyone all right?" Fliw held up his hands and his rescuers gradually quietened down.

"We are not yet safe comrades. We must leave this place with all haste before The Something returns." There was an immediate silence, everyone had been concentrating on Schwartzkopf and the whereabouts of the vile entity had not been uppermost in their minds.

"Was that the witch we heard?" asked Clarissa, unable to contain herself. Fliw nodded and gestured that they should all move quickly from the room.

"Where is she now?" asked Brett as they hurried out into the corridor.

"I have banished her from this place. She will trouble us no more, but the effort has weakened me. Brett, I will need both your and Casey's help if I am to reach the safety of my home." Brett immediately went to the hermit's aid and supported him. In fact he carried Fliw's small frame with ease lifting him from the floor, his staff dragging behind them.

"Take care young friends, we do not know where The Something is right now." With this warning ringing in their ears, they made slow progress as they retraced their steps up the staircase and out into the courtyard.

It was still raining hard and the wind was whipping each drop into a tiny missile and hurling it at the small intrepid party.

"This is awful," wailed Clarissa, desperately trying to keep her wet hair out of her eyes.

"No it's worse," squeaked Twinkle. "We'll never get all the way home at this rate." Tommy had to agree and as they went to meet Casey back at the drawbridge, he could bear it no longer.

"Oh, horrid weather, I really wish the wind would die down and the rain would ease off," he raised his arms to the sky and shouted the words into the wind. Slowly the wind eased and the raindrops became smaller and less vicious. The party stopped and all looked at Tommy. "What?" he cried.

"Why on earth didn't you do that on the way in stupid?" Clarissa was beside herself. Tommy just looked at her. He had to admit that would have been by far the most sensible thing to do. Brett laughed, at least one of them had kept their sense of humour.

"That would have made the task far too easy though, pretty lady." Clarissa looked at Brett and then at the rest of the company. Was she the only sane person here? It appeared so at this moment, but for some reason she nodded and fell into step by Bretts' side.

"I was more than worried about you folks. There was great, mighty flashes and bangs coming from where you went to and I was a thinkin' that you'd met your ends down there." Casey addressed the group. Tommy went up to him.

"But you kept to your post Casey and that's the mark of a real soldier." Casey stood proudly at the edge of the drawbridge and showed them all safely across. When he saw Brett with Fliw, he immediately motioned that he should take Fliw's other arm and leave his staff redundant. Brett nodded and between them they supported the elderly mortal as they travelled. Each of the company noticed this action, but chose not to draw attention to the frail figure resting between two sturdy fellows. They marched steadily on for a few minutes before anyone could think of something to say. It was Twinkle who broke the silence.

"Shall we all have some hot chocolate and cake when we get to Fliw's house?" she enquired. This was half out of hospitality and trying to deflect attention from Fliw and half from the sudden thought that she might not have to miss out on Fliw's rather good cake. Fliw seemed to rally round to this suggestion.

"I think," he announced, "that this is by far the most sensible idea that a little fairy has ever had in this world. I extend the invitation to each of you in our merry band." This lifted their spirits somewhat and they began to move slightly more quickly than before.

Without the rest of the friends noticing, Fliw was becoming very weary and Brett and Casey were mostly carrying his tired frame. Casey looked across at Brett and they mutually agreed without speaking that they should carry Fliw the rest of the way.

Chapter 20

Within the hour, they arrived at Fliw's house. The wind had subsided and the rain had turned to drizzle. Tommy, Clarissa and Twinkle went forward and surveyed the damage that had been inflicted upon the front door. There was a morass of singed wood and door hinge scattered inside and out, but the remainder of the structure appeared intact. Twinkle and Clarissa went inside first, they appeared to have no fear of the interior. If anyone had asked them they would have said that they felt they had to be of some use to the company. Both girls went into the kitchen and began to prepare the hot chocolate and cake that Twinkle had begun to prepare so many hours before.

Tommy entered the house and stood in the centre of the front room. He surveyed the scene as Brett and Casey carried Fliw into the room and placed him carefully in his armchair. Fliw seemed to appreciate the fact that he had been brought home and he smiled and nodded as he heard the girls busily preparing refreshments. He sank back into the chair and closed his eyes. Brett and Casey quietly joined Tommy and they surveyed the scene.

"What do we do about the door?" whispered Tommy.

"Don't rightly know," replied Casey.

"Where's Hoy-Paloy?" whispered Brett and they all looked quickly around. He was nowhere to be seen, this worried Tommy, surely he wouldn't abandon his master when he so clearly needed help?

"Here," said a very quiet Hoy-Paloy. He had been outside the front door sifting through the damage. "What can we do about this then?" he eyed the rubble and the mess strewn across the front room.

"Leave it," said Fliw and they all turned to face him. "I'll deal with it in the morning." At this point Twinkle returned to the room.

"What've I missed?" she enquired, looking at the solemn faces. Hoy-Paloy pointed sadly at the doorway. Twinkle grinned from ear to ear. "I've always wanted to swap that dowdy old door," she announced and went to stand near to the door frame. With a flick of her wand she aimed a spurt of sparkly fairy dust in the direction of the hole. Unfortunately it didn't quite reach and pansies began to grow out of Fliws' floor. Hoy-Paloy put his head in his hands.

"Oh that foolish fairy. What have I done to deserve this?" Tommy put his hand on Hoy-Paloy's arm.

"Give her a chance. Twinkle stand a bit closer and have another go." Twinkle took a deep breath and two steps closer to the space in front of her. She lifted her wand high above her head and swept it forcefully down toward the door. Her wings stuck straight out behind her and she was standing right on the very points of her ballet shoes. Clarissa had wandered back into the room and she joined the others and they all willed Twinkle to have a successful spell.

The fairy dust that sprang from the tip of Twinkle's wand sparkled brighter than before and it whirled around the aperture where the door had once been. As they stood and watched in amazement, slowly a pale pink door began to appear. It was a wooden door and quite robust by the look of the grain, but as they watched a pattern began to develop upon the pale pink paint. The pattern became clearer and they all stood and admired the prettiest garland of pansies they had ever seen. Hoy-Paloy groaned again.

"Twinkle this is a boys house, not your house." Twinkle was out of breath now, this spell was the hardest she had ever done and the effort she had put into it now seemed wasted. A deep chuckling interrupted the proceedings and they all turned to see who thought this was funny. The chuckle turned into a giggle and then into a deep roar and the culprit was Fliw. How he laughed and through the tears rolling down his face he said to Twinkle.

"You leave that door where it is young fairy. I'm proud of you and it is a very pretty door." Everyone smiled at this, it was the most positive thing they had seen Fliw do for quite some time and they had all been quite concerned about him.

After a while, when they had stopped laughing, Fliw spoke again.

"I could really do with some sleep now and I'm sure that you two," he gestured toward Tommy and Clarissa "will need your sleep before tomorrow."

Tommy raised his eyebrows.

"Why? What's happening tomorrow?"

But Fliw did not respond and filled with curiosity they left the house with Hoy-Paloy to return from The Kingdom.

As they stepped forward into the gateway, Clarissa was convinced she saw something out of the corner of her eye and she had a very peculiar feeling in the bottom of her stomach. Quickly she reached for Hoy-Paloy's hand and she noticed that Tommy had done the same. Hoy-Paloy had a very serious air about him and he set quite fast pace as they walked along.

"Now sing, and mind you sing loud and strong," he instructed. "There are strange things afoot this night." The three of them held hands tightly and sang with all their might;

"Hoy-Paloy is on his way.

He has a task to do this day.

Fliw the mystic made me this charm.

The purpose of which is to keep us from harm.

Pretty flowers and forests too.

Can we save them? Tommy, it's up to you."

It was fair to say that they were nearly sprinting as they appeared in Tommy's room and both Tommy and Clarissa were out of breath.

"Will you be all right on the way back Hoy-Paloy?" asked Clarissa. She had grown quite fond of this unfortunate little creature and his eyes shone as he nodded and said.

"I shall be fine young lady. Thank you for your concern." He bowed deeply, his beard once more touching the floor. With that he opened the bedroom door and quietly tiptoed out onto the landing.

"He will be OK, won't he?" asked Clarissa. Tommy shook his head slowly.

"I've no idea. I hope so, but we won't if we don't clear up this mess of mud." Clarissa looked at where Tommy pointed and to her horror their boots were caked in sloppy red mud and their footprints were clear on the carpet. These clear prints led from the fireplace to where they now stood. Her face fell and they both hurried to take off their boots.

"Tell you what," she whispered, "we're probably better off leaving this to dry and getting up very early to brush it off when it's dried." Tommy nodded. "Although we will have to clean our boots now." They did this as quietly as possible and hurried out of their outer garments and slipped quietly into their beds.

Chapter 21

The scene was set. The fate of the two worlds possibly even the universe depended on an eleven-year-old boy. This was no ordinary little boy though. He had never bullied any little children at school, he was kind and considerate to older people, he handed his homework in on time and did everything his mother asked. Other children at school committed mischief and offences against society but Tommy would never be part of that. He was a model son to every mother and father in fact the perfect choice for Fliw.

Tommy's training had, given the time available, gone extremely well. His young age and open mind had made it far easier for Fliw. However, Fliw guarded a deep secret surrounding Tommy's past. He knew one day he may have to reveal it, but for the time being, that secret must remain with him. No matter how many times he thought and tried to reassure himself that Tommy was ready to take on such responsibility, somehow there was just a little doubt in his mind.

The last few days had taken their toll on a very old man. Fliw had almost paid the ultimate price for the weakness in his power. If Tommy was as receptive as Fliw predicted then he would soon accomplish his mission. All he required Tommy to do was to hold the barrier around the gateway for one day. Afterwards Fliw could draw on his powers in the future if required. The one-day's respite would be sufficient for Fliw to recuperate to his maximum strength and continue guarding the gateway.

At the back of his mind however was the recent encounter with Schwartzkopf. That had been extremely worrying for Fliw, and dangerous. It may have been an opportunity to test Tommy in a real life situation without Fliw's help, but only Fliw realised how close calamity had come. He muttered under his breath.

"Don't know how long I could have held out, getting tired, old…" Fliw's doubt was still there. Would Tommy be up to the challenge at such a young age, and with training at a minimum? His mind wandered back to the time when he was chosen to take the Arch-Druid's role. His mentor gave him a rigorous training schedule many times longer than that afforded to Tommy. Fliw developed his powers over a much longer period and was not even chosen until his sixteenth birthday, five years later than Tommy.

"Too many variables," he uttered "Have to judge him on what I've seen so far, cannot leave it any longer. The Something's power increases daily."

Schwartzkopf had been banished. It was an early victory for Fliw and Tommy, and he could not allow Tommy to become overconfident. If The Something begins an assault on the gateway then it is the druid's responsibility to protect it with their life. What he couldn't predict was when the likely assault would take place. Would it be today? Tomorrow? Next year?

Fliw's thoughts were suddenly interrupted by the appearance of Twinkle.

"Hello Fliw, how are you? Oh! I see from your expression, not too happy," her entrance became more punctuated as she tripped over a loose floorboard catapulting her whole body through space. Twinkle's landing was not at all lady-like, she landed in a heap of pink satin and lace at Fliw's feet. Although her dignity had been compromised, Twinkle soon recovered and lifted herself back to her feet, brushed herself down and rearranged her clothing. Underneath her pink tutu she revealed matching pink knickers and a pink vest, not at all the position in which a fairy should find herself.

"Oops sorry Fliw, how clumsy of me," she tried to regain a vertical position. "Oh and look what I've done to my wand!" She held up her right hand to reveal a rather bent stick that copied the contour of her belly. "Now I will have to use my spare wand until this is fixed. Are you any better Fliw?"

"I am as well as can be expected under the circumstances Twinkle. My last encounter with Schwartzkopf set me back to a point of grave concern."

"What can I do to help?" Twinkle asked.

"Thank you Twinkle, you know I respect your powers however limited they are. I don't want to hurt your feelings but the ability to make flowers grow into pretty colours is not quite the power that is required to control The Something." Twinkle's smile quickly turned into a frown in disappointment at her abilities. "But I'm really glad to have you on my team, your help has always been invaluable." The frown quickly returned to a smile and remained receptive to those few kind words from Fliw. The embarrassment of falling over had been forgotten.

"Twinkle, I need you to find Hoy-Paloy for me quickly then ask Brett and Casey to join us as soon as possible."

"Is there something wrong Fliw?"

"Something is the problem Twinkle. I fear now Schwartzkopf is defeated and in my weakened state it gives The Something the opportunity to move towards the gateway and we all know what will happen if we allow that."

"Oh, Oh… Ohhhh." Trying to find the right words to respond Twinkle accepted the responsibility. "Yes of course. I will go right now this minute with your message." Without any further conversation Twinkle changed herself into a bright light the size of a tennis ball and flew out of Fliw's window on her mission.

At Hoy-Paloy's cave Twinkle assumed her full size and again in her eagerness stumbled into Hoy-Paloy's cave head first. Lying prostrate on the dusty floor she began to retell the message that Fliw had entrusted with her.

"Hoy-Paloy, Hoy-Paloy, quickly you must go to Fliw he needs you on a mission. He's sent me to find Brett and Casey I must go now time is of the essence," she once again changed into a bright light and disappeared back through the cave entrance. Hoy-Paloy in double quick time made his way down the path towards Fliw's house, expecting the worst. He hummed the familiar verse without uttering the words, he had too much on his mind to do anything else.

Within thirty minutes he arrived out of breath at Fliw's house, the doorway still bedecked with pansies.

"Yes Fliw. You wanted me urgently?" he enquired as he entered.

"Ah yes. Thank you Hoy-Paloy, you need to bring Tommy back again to The Kingdom. I think the time has arrived when we can expect The Something to move towards the gateway." Fliw had just about finished his words when Hoy-Paloy disappeared out of the door heading back to his cave. He retrieved his keys from the invisible casket and unlocked the door to Tommy's world emerging from the fireplace once again.

"Tommy, Tommy wake up, wake up. Fliw wants you urgently." A rather dazed young man gradually extracted himself from under the duvet.

"Oh what's wrong now Hoy-Paloy? Not again, how many times tonight?"

"Quickly Tommy. You have to come now." Tommy was responding to the request but the urgency did not seem to register. Eyes almost closed, Tommy floundered around the room in darkness trying to dress himself.

"Quickly. Quickly, Tommy." Hoy-Paloy urged him. "Time is of the essence."

"Right, I'm ready let's go." It was almost a written invitation to Clarissa who knocked on the door and entered Tommy's bedroom.

"I heard voices is that Hoy-Paloy?" she asked.

"Yes, it's me Clarissa. Tommy has been summoned by Fliw back to The Kingdom – urgently."

"Oh right. I'll get dressed immediately, please wait for me." Clarissa returned within minutes respectfully attired and complete with her pony crop.

"Right, let's go." Both Hoy-Paloy and Tommy responded by moving out of the bedroom to the grandfather clock. Hoy-Paloy removed the small golden key from around his neck and inserted it into the lock. Once again, the door appeared and the trio made their way into The Kingdom and appeared in Hoy-Paloy's living room. He dutifully replaced the golden keys into the casket which disappeared as soon as the lid was closed.

"Onward to Fliw's house," instructed Hoy-Paloy "We must not waste any more time."

Twinkle had in the meantime located Brett and Casey urging them to meet as soon as possible at Fliw's house. Casey was the first to arrive parking his engine neatly outside the house, quickly followed by Twinkle.

"Have the others arrived yet?" she enquired.

"Not yet Twinkle, I'm expecting them very shortly." No sooner had Fliw uttered these words when Brett floated in.

"What's the score then folks? Good guys ten: Bad guys nil?"

"Be patient Brett, I will explain when everyone has arrived but it will be no surprise to you." The group welcomed the arrival of Hoy-Paloy, Tommy and Clarissa.

"Glad to see you folks again, seems like only a few hours since we saw you." This was from Casey.

"It's less than that," Tommy muttered, still with sleep in his eyes.

"Thank you all for coming, I'm afraid the time may be close. The Something may move on the gateway soon and we must prepare." The seriousness of the situation reflected in his face. Clarissa looked at Tommy expecting him to say something but a response was not forthcoming.

"What's the plan Fliw?" Twinkle asked.

"I've no right to ask your help in this matter. I don't want to put any of you at risk, this problem remains a druid problem." Silence filled the room until Hoy-Paloy was first to respond.

"I am the gatekeeper, responsible for the golden keys and have been for many centuries and my place is with Fliw." Twinkle responded next.

"My powers may not be great but they are yours to command Fliw."

"Whatever you want me to do Fliw, I shall help with what I can." Brett responded.

"Ya can count on me too." Casey nodded in approval.

"Thank you all my friends. Thank you."

"Ahem – What about us?" Clarissa enquired.

"Ah yes, our friends from the other world. Without you two it would be impossible to tackle The Something." Clarissa slapped the pony crop against her thigh in agreement and Tommy nodded his approval.

Fliw began to outline his plan to protect the gateway. It was a simple plan but one that should work given the odds against them. It was to be in three parts a defensive move, a distracting move and then an assault to eradicate the threat. It all sounded very tactical and high level to the group, however they had absolute faith in Fliw whatever his plans.

Fliw would initially take the lead. He would provide the defensive assault against The Something. Twinkle, Casey and Brett would then converge on The Something and distract it in any way they could think. Finally Tommy would provide the main assault with help from Fliw.

"But you've left me out Fliw!" Hoy-Paloy interrupted.

"No. I need you to stand guard over the casket that contains the golden keys. If our efforts fail, Hoy-Paloy, it's up to you my friend as the gatekeeper to destroy the casket. Without the keys The Something will be unable to move between our worlds but that can only be temporary. I am sure it would only be a matter of time before it is able to use the gateway without the keys. After that, then all existence in both worlds would cease followed by the rest of the universe."

The story sounded more frightening than ever before. The protection provided by Fliw had shielded everyone from danger in the past and that danger was now becoming all too apparent.

"Each of you must remember that one powerful weapon The Something has is the ability to make you believe your worst fears. Over the years I've grown immune to such thoughts but if we are in direct conflict with it then you will all be vulnerable. Your defence is in your mind. Block out the unreal and focus on the threat."

"All sounds very confusing," muttered Casey. "No one makes me think anything I don't want to."

"Casey, what do you think of this?" joked Brett.

"Hmmph," retorted Casey.

"Well, my friends, I sense the time is near, shall we go to face the evil head on?" The group trailed out of Fliw's house and walked towards the castle. As the light began to disappear Fliw raised his right hand.

"This is where we part company. You all know what to do and all I can say is thank you for your support, my friends." Fliw continued to walk towards the castle leaving the group to organise themselves.

"Right," said Tommy, "we all know what to do, Hoy-Paloy off you go and guard outside your cave."

"My home, please Tommy."

"Sorry Hoy-Paloy, I stand corrected, I meant your home." Hoy-Paloy waved goodbye to everyone and headed toward the cave singing his rhyme in an attempt to cheer himself up.

"Hoy-Paloy is on his way.

He has a task to do this day.

Fliw the mystic made me this charm.

The purpose of which is to keep us from harm.

Pretty flowers and forests too.

Can we save them? Tommy, it's up to you."

"Next Casey, Brett and Twinkle, position yourselves behind those trees over there as far apart as possible. If The Something gets past Fliw its up to you three to distract it and whilst that happens I will attempt to fight it."

"What about me then?" asked Clarissa. "What is my function?"

"Yes, that whip of yours is quite lethal isn't it? If The Something defeats me then whip it to death!" Twinkle, Brett and Casey took up their positions as instructed whilst Tommy and Clarissa waited impatiently. Fliw disappeared over the brow of the hill.

Chapter 22

Fliw continued his journey in the direction of The Something's castle, expecting at any minute to confront his worst nightmare. He became aware that the birds were no longer singing, and no animals walked the forest. What had been so far a sunny day, was gradually turning into semi-darkness. A cold chill of fear began to engulf him. He stood quite still. The end of his staff was positioned firmly on the ground, his grip around it revealed the whites of his knuckles.

There before him, as large as life, was The Something. It was a gaseous smoky apparition standing five metres high and across. At last he stood before his foe, determined not to give ground and defeat it once and for all.

"Back to your castle and remain there forever," he commanded. Then slowly but surely the cloud began to move and a face took shape in its centre. The face too menacing to describe, leered at Fliw for a few seconds then bellowed.

"Your time has come Fliw, your power has almost gone. I shall swat you like a fly. Soon both worlds will know The Something is all powerful."

There was not a sound. The birds and animals had long since fled. Not even the rustle of the trees broke the silence. A huge crack echoed across the fields where they both stood. Within a millisecond a lightning bolt danced just centimetres in front of Fliw's feet, unable to penetrate the invisible screen around him.

"No invisible screen will protect you old man. My power is greater." A second third and fourth bolt of lightening struck, each failing to hit its target.

Next came two huge boulders at least ten tonnes each in weight and travelling at the speed of sound. The impact was incredible. Both boulders hit Fliw and instantly disintegrated into powder from the force but still Fliw stood his ground. That ground soon disappeared from under him, leaving a pit that looked bottomless. Fliw levitated above the pit, steady as a rock waiting for the next skirmish.

Two titans appeared in front and behind Fliw towering a hundred metres high, wielding clubs the size of huge oak trees. The blows were crushing and devastating and Fliw began to sink to his knees from the onslaught. His power was weakening and The Something sensed victory.

The pit began to crack and the ground gave way to an earthquake. Gradually Fliw began to sink between its jaws whilst the titans continued their battering. Fliw waved his staff and the titans disappeared into oblivion but the earth had by this time swallowed him. He was nowhere to be seen. At last The Something had removed its mortal enemy for good.

It continued its journey across the fields surrounding the castle moving across the place that Fliw had disappeared. The face on the cloud of fear had now disappeared and it had resumed its original state. Grass, flowers and anything living died instantly the moment they were touched, leaving a trail of devastation to nature behind. Animals sensed the danger and fled for their lives knowing that to touch it would mean instant death.

The Something rolled over the brow of the hill Fliw had earlier passed as he said good bye to his friends. A deadly silence preceded its journey, forming a tell-tale sign and warning to all living things.

"Here it comes," announced Twinkle, fear emanating from her voice.

"Get ready you two," shouted Casey. "I will go first to distract it. Brett, you follow me." Casey's engine was now at maximum steam pressure, a great big belching power horse ready for battle. Its wheels skidded on the green pasture but soon found traction and speed. Casey shovelled more fuel into its firebox and closed the plate, heading directly for The Something from a westerly direction. Thirty, forty, fifty, sixty kilometres per hour – he continued to gather momentum as the engine drew closer to The Something.

Although the noise broke the silence of the day, The Something did not become aware of any threat from Casey. His westerly approach had seemed to work tactically. Their enemy had not realised the danger until it was too late. Casey careered through the entity. Although its appearance was cloud-like, the cry of pain was real. A sixty tonne engine at seventy kilometres per hour makes a formidable battering ram and lethal weapon.

Brett spotted an opportunity and began his move but from an easterly direction. He had adapted his anti-gravity vehicle's intake to simulate a vacuum. Anything that was sucked into the power unit would be instantly shredded to oblivion. Approaching the Something from the setting sun he appeared invisible to the naked eye and therefore, like Casey, had an immediate advantage.

The scream of pain this time was quite profound. It echoed across the battlefield as Casey's battering ram ran right through The Something. Clearly some damage had been done but to what extent no one could assess. Three lightning bolts struck Casey's engine side on, slicing the fuel box clearly from its coupling. The engine turned to react to the attack, resulting in another lightning bolt battering the engine. Casey once again steered it toward The Something, this time from a southerly direction but his enemy was now fully aware of the danger.

The entity began to take on the face used in its encounter with Fliw. Its frightening appearance had no effect on its attackers and by now Brett was close to his foe. Brett's AG vehicle hit the extremity of The Something, its vacuum sucking in its very essence. Another scream resulted from the onslaught as its very fibre disappeared into the AG vehicle.

By now it was apparent to The Something and its attackers that Fliw, although he had disappeared into the earth, had managed to remove the barrier that protected his foe, leaving the way clear for Casey, Brett and Twinkle. Although this was a big advantage the power of the entity still remained. The entity turned in reaction to Brett's AG vehicle as once again Casey hit his foe from a southerly direction. This time his speed was well over eighty kilometres per hour.

Twinkle spotted her opportunity to move and changed into a small ball of light flying directly at the entity. Another scream of pain reverberated around the scene as Casey once again connected with The Something. At the same time Brett sucked more of the cloud into his AG vehicle, followed by another scream of pain.

A mountain suddenly erupted from the ground in front of Casey. It was too late to apply the brakes. The engine smashed into a rock face catapulting Casey from the controls. His engine boilers bursting into a huge cloud of steam ending any more threat to The Something. At the same time Twinkle distracted it away from Casey to avoid any more harm to her friend. This manoeuvre only put her into danger as the cloud enveloped her bright ball of light.

Once again Brett ploughed into his enemy causing more pain, however this time revenge was waiting to meet him. A huge tidal wave hit him head-on. He never saw it coming. The power of the wave parted him from his AG vehicle extinguishing the engine and Brett was nowhere to be seen, but he no longer posed a threat to The Something.

Twinkle continued to use her speed to out manoeuvre the entity, its size was an advantage to her but she proved to be only a minor threat. The Something continued to advance toward Hoy-Paloy's cave and the gateway. It was Tommy's turn next. He was the last hope for both worlds but he faced the challenge like a hero.

"Tommy be careful, it looks dangerous out there," said Clarissa.

"Don't worry, Fliw taught me well and I won't let him down." Tommy walked out in front of the terror cloud, hiding any fear that he felt. It stopped only metres away from him and the cloud swirled furiously for several minutes.

"Ahh… You are the young druid that is to succeed Fliw. How puny you are, I shall squash you like a fly. Fliw the hermit was no match for me and neither are you. Once you are disposed of nothing will stand in my way."

"You big bully. Don't you dare hurt my friend, or you'll have to deal with me!" pronounced Clarissa, slapping the side of her leg with the pony whip. A gust of wind strong enough to knock her off her feet erupted from the entity, sending her flying most un-lady-like into the undergrowth.

"Nobody hurts my friends. You're a big bully and I hate bullies!" Tommy levitated himself to a height whereby he towered above his enemy. He disappeared from sight and only a voice could be heard. The face of

The Something for the first time looked puzzled and concerned at the new foe in front of him (or so he thought). A huge ball of fire streamed from nowhere toward the last place Tommy had been. At one thousand degrees centigrade the heat would instantly vaporise anything living, but Tommy was not in its path. The fire consumed the forest and all that lived there, everything was burnt to a crisp.

"Where are you mini-human being? You can't hide from me for long." Frustration was building up in The Something. Frustration and anger the ingredients of making mistakes. A huge bubble enveloped the cloud, a bubble of indestructible construction. Immediately The Something began to pound the sides of the container, unable to break free. Tommy reappeared behind his foe, proud of his first attempt to immobilise the threat before him.

Three titans suddenly appeared, each carrying formidable weapons of destruction. They systematically began to smash the dome that held their master prisoner. Each strike was enough to shatter a brick house but the structure never cracked. The titans realised their efforts were in vain and they turned on Tommy from all sides in a pincer movement. His head spun as he tried to concentrate on the danger all around him. Concentration was paramount to ensure the integrity of the prison surrounding The Something.

The first titan swung a huge hammer at least a tonne in weight towards Tommy, quickly followed by a second and third. Tommy waved his hand and the hammers locked in position a short distance above him. The titans froze in their footsteps unable to move a muscle until the ground underneath them opened up and swallowed them in one movement. What Tommy had not expected was the mini-tornado advancing on him from behind. It was a complete surprise when it hit him and he was swept away in its iron grip. Concentration was lost, the shield around The Something disappeared and it continued to advance on the gateway. Only Hoy-Paloy stood between the threat of The Something to both worlds. Devastation was only minutes away.

Suddenly the earth opened up and a canyon formed, the tear in the ground stretched a kilometre across. The Grand Canyon in America was dwarfed by what lay before The Something. From its centre emerged Tommy, his hair slightly dishevelled from the mini-tornado and he hovered in front of his adversary.

"Stop right there and go no further," he commanded. A huge bellowing laugh echoed throughout the canyon.

"Puny mortal, how can you still be alive? A million volts of energy will dispose of you." Within milliseconds a hundred lightning bolts rained on Tommy, only to rebound back on the entity with equal force. For the first time since The Something advanced toward the gateway, Tommy saw it move backwards. Clearly either Tommy's new defensive move had worked or The Something was losing its power. If that was the case, then Fliw's plan was working well and it gave Tommy the encouragement he needed.

Once again he levitated himself across the canyon to the edge and faced The Something head-on. Only metres separated the mighty powers.

"You will pay for that dearly," said The Something.

"Get back to your castle, evil being, and never darken this land again."

"Foolish mortal, did you think mere lightning bolts could destroy one as powerful as me?"

"No, but this might." Behind The Something appeared

yet another hole in the ground. This one used the natural forces of nature to create a powerful down draft into a bottomless pit. The suction caught hold of the wispy end of the evil cloud, dragging it toward an indestructible prison.

"No, no, no," it cried. The suction was so powerful it tore surrounding mighty oaks effortlessly from their roots and they disappeared into the vortex. Abject terror echoed in the voice of The Something as it screeched abuse at Tommy. As solid as a rock, he held his concentration and focused on the task in hand, determined that nothing would distract him.

"Tommy, Tommy Tommy Ravensdale, are you not listening to me?" screeched a familiar voice.

"Ravensdale, Ravensdale's a big girls' blouse."

"Nancy Ravensdale is daydreaming again." More familiar voices. The distraction was too much he had to turn away from The Something to look behind him. It was Miss Tonge and the bullies Ian, Rick and Dave from school, how could they have found their way into this world?

"Why Miss Tonge. What are you doing here?" Tommy could feel his grasp on reality slipping away.

"You've been daydreaming again, haven't you, and ignoring your lessons? Won't you ever learn? I've told you time and time again you must concentrate more." The bullies then began to taunt Tommy in the usual fashion, demanding his dinner money with menaces.

"No, I won't give it to you," he muttered. "Go away."

"Give us your money or we'll tie you up to the bike shed," demanded Ian Robertson. The idiot Mounter who was always a couple of butties short of a picnic repeated the phrase.

"Erm, give us, er give us, what was it?" he asked.

Rick Priestley said bullishly,

"Yer money jerk!" Whilst this distraction was going on The Something advanced towards Tommy once again in a terrifying and menacing manner. Tommy's apprehension grew as the four characters bombarded him with threats and abuse until he heard a familiar voice whisper in his ear.

"Remember Tommy, The Something has the power to create your worst nightmare."

"Of course!" he shouted. "You are just figments of my imagination. Go," he demanded. "Go now." As quickly as they had appeared, Miss Tonge and the bullies disappeared into a puff of smoke but it was too late, the distraction had worked and The Something surrounded him in its evil cloud. Tommy was firmly held inside the choking cloud. There was no beginning and no end and no apparent way out. He became concerned and his concern became a worry and then his worry was rapidly developing into panic. The responsibility he carried was beginning to take hold.

"Tommy, Tommy, remember your powers. Let them guide you out of danger." It was Fliw, again whispering advice into his ear. Inspired once again by the words of his mentor, Tommy concentrated on freeing himself from the grip of the cloud and finding his way out. Within minutes he emerged outside the cloud in front of The Something and ready for the final showdown.

"You puny creature, what do I have to do to dispose of you? I shall swat you once again." The ground underneath Tommy liquefied into a superglue type of substance fixing his feet firmly to the ground. From all four points of the compass came four sixty-tonne steam engines at breakneck speed all converging on the centre point and that point was Tommy.

'There is no way out,' he thought. 'In five seconds I'll be mincemeat, no time to work out an escape route. All is lost and I have failed'.

Like a hero out of a movie Twinkle appeared in the nick of time, racing towards her friend swooping out of the sky.

"I'm here Tommy, grab hold of my hand." And like a well planned rescue, Tommy was lifted out of his shoes by Twinkle. An instant later the four trains converged at seventy kilometres per hour in a devastating crash. Smoke cleared and once again Tommy faced head-on The Something. The bottomless pit opened up yet further and began to suck The Something into its murky depths. The power of the suction increased as a wild scream came from the vanishing Something. It was a matter of seconds before the bottomless pit had swallowed the whole entity. Immediately it had disappeared a huge rock cap came smashing down to plug the hole, a fitting prison for one so evil.

Tommy fell to the ground exhausted from his ordeal but not letting his power diminish on The Something's imprisonment. His mind turned to his friends. What had happened to them? Had they survived or not? Next, as if he had willed it to happen, Twinkle appeared and said,

"That was a close call, you've done it Tommy. You've imprisoned The Something. Fliw would be proud of you."

"Twinkle, oh I'm so glad to see you. What happened to Brett and Casey?" Then again as if it was stage managed, Brett came skating along in his AG vehicle and Casey's steam engine screeched to a halt. "Brett, Casey I'm so glad you're all right I was so worried."

"There's no need to worry little hero. We're OK, how are you?"

"Yes, yes I'm fine," replied Tommy.

"And so am I little man," a familiar voice butted in.

"Clarissa, don't call me little man. You know I hate it!"

"Yes, I'm fine, thank you Tommy," was her indignant response.

"I'm glad to see all of you. But what of Fliw, has anyone seen him?" They all sadly shook their heads and then solemnly looked toward the ground in a sign of respect. By this time Hoy-Paloy had joined them, already aware of the result of The Something's challenge.

"What's the matter with you all? You should be celebrating the defeat of The Something, not looking as if you've been to a funeral."

"We may have lost Fliw," Tommy replied.

"Fliw?" questioned Hoy-Paloy.

"Yes, the ground swallowed him up and we've not seen him since."

"No. No, no, no, Fliw's OK."

"He is? He is!" they all joined in

"How do you know Hoy-Paloy?" questioned Clarissa.

"How do I know?" said Hoy-Paloy. "Because he's standing behind you as large as life."

They all instantly turned on their heels at Hoy-Paloy's statement and to their amazement there was Fliw as large as life, just as Hoy-Paloy had told them.

"Fliw!" they all shouted in unison. "You're all right."

"Yes, thank you for your concern. I was temporarily out of action because my powers had almost faded away. But thanks to Tommy I'm now on my way to recovery." They all began to celebrate by joining in with Hoy-Paloy's favourite rhyme:

"Hoy-Paloy is on his way.

He has a task to do this day.

Fliw the mystic made me this charm.

The purpose of which is to keep us from harm.
Pretty flowers and forests too.
Can we save them? Tommy, it's up to you."

The celebrations lasted for a whole day. The birds and animals had returned and The Kingdom had been restored to its former glory. Tommy and Clarissa bid everyone farewell and it was time to return to their own world. Fliw had shaken Tommy's hand and wished him well for the future, then bade Hoy-Paloy to return both him and Clarissa through the gateway.

"Cheerio," said Tommy, "see you again sometime."

"And the same applies to me," said Clarissa. Within minutes, Hoy-Paloy had delivered them back through the gateway and into Tommy's bedroom.

"I'm going straight to bed Tommy, and I suggest you do the same." Tommy obediently responded to Clarissa's suggestion. She left for her bedroom and then Tommy retired with his dreams, peaceful in the knowledge that he had successfully answered 'the question'.

Chapter 23

Tommy got into his Dad's car and immediately looked out of the back window. Clarissa and Martha stood on the top step and Clarissa waved in an unsure fashion. Tommy waved back, and turned to face the front. Strapping his seat belt tightly around him he could not believe what had happened to him in the past few days. He had met so many wonderful people and experienced so many unusual things that it could not all be over so suddenly, could it? He turned back as his Dad got into the driver's seat and gasped at what he saw. Behind the two girls and just to one side he was sure he could see Hoy-Paloy peering out of the front door and waving. He waved back and the two girls thought he was waving at them and so they waved until the car pulled out of the gates and onto the road. Tommy turned and regained his seat. He had an awful lot to think about on the way back to his mother.

Presently his Dad spoke.

"So, how do you like staying with us, was it good?" Tommy shrugged.

"It was all right," he responded, not wanting to get into a deep conversation about why he had liked being there.

"Clarissa's OK when you get to know her though, isn't she?" Tommy shrugged, he was desperate not to show any enthusiasm. He felt suddenly guilty that he had such a good time and all week his poor mother had been at home alone worrying about him. They spent the rest of the journey chatting about Alton Towers and Stonehenge and everything else that they had done. His Dad didn't ask any more about how he felt and this was a great relief to Tommy.

It was around four in the afternoon when they pulled up outside Tommy's house and there was a strange car in the driveway. As they stopped, Tommy's Mum came out and ran to the back door of the car.

"Tommy. How have you been? Was it good? How did you like your holiday?" Tommy was not expecting this, he had missed his Mum but had not expected her to have been so concerned. This made him feel slightly worse as he had such a good time. Tommy scrambled out of the back door of the car and grabbed his suitcase as his Dad handed it to him.

There was a pause and Tommy felt an urge to hug his Dad as now he had no idea when he would see him again. Instead he looked at him and said,

"Thank you for having me. I really enjoyed myself." Tommy's parents looked at each other and smiled knowingly. David got back into his car and drove slowly away. Tommy waited by the gate and waved until he couldn't see him any more. He turned and walked back to the door where his mother stood. She welcomed him in and closed the door behind them.

"Did you have a good time dear?" she asked. Tommy nodded and he felt even worse, he had a good time whilst she had been here all on her own. His mother bent and kissed him on the forehead and he felt as if he had returned home from a great journey. As he followed her into the lounge he noticed someone else sitting in the chair by the front window and he stopped suddenly.

"Tommy, this is Brandon. He's my friend and he came to keep me company whilst you were at your Dad's." Tommy looked from one to the other and stood for ages without saying anything. This wasn't fair, he'd spent the last week feeling guilty because he was wrapped up in some amazing adventure when all the time his mother had been quite all right. He could have enjoyed himself more if he had known. This flashed through his mind and at the same time he contemplated whether he would have even tried to like Clarissa and Martha if he had known about this new friend. His head was spinning and he knew he had not spoken for quite a few minutes. Then 'Brandon' spoke.

"Hey little man. How do you fancy coming to my place with your Mum and riding on my Go-Karts?" Tommy was dumbfounded, he was convinced he was not supposed to like any of what was happening but this was his dream come true. He nodded slowly and Brandon stood up and walked toward him.

Tommy's eyes widened as the guy stood up, it was like he was experiencing something from a dream. This guy was in stature and mannerisms an exact replica of Brett Trailblazer, with whom he had experienced so much over the past few days.

"Brett?" he gasped. The guy hesitated.

"No. Brandon." He said the name slowly and put out his hand for Tommy to shake. Tommy took it and as he shook it he enquired,

"So, these Go-Karts, are they like the anti-gravity ones in the new PC game?" Brandon shook his head and pulled a bag out of his pocket.

"Here. I got this for you." He handed the bag to Tommy who took it and ripped out the contents. To his great amazement it was the new game whose starring competitor was Brett Trailblazer. He held the case up for Brandon to see.

"There, Brett Trailblazer," he announced, "and you

look just like him." Brandon stooped down and crouched next to Tommy.

"Can we be friends?" he asked.

"Wow! Just wait 'till I show this to Clarissa, she won't believe it." Tommy looked at his mother, expecting her to look sad. "Sorry Mum," he said.

"No dear, you're allowed to like her you know. After all, you are step-brother and sister and I don't want you to feel bad. There's enough room in all of our lives for Clarissa, Martha, your Dad, Brandon and for you. We all love you very much and we want you to be happy." Tommy scowled, he had too much information now and it was not what he had expected at all.

At this point the telephone rang and Tommy's Mum went to answer it. Tommy listened to the conversation and paid half-attention to Brandon explaining how the Go-Karting worked. For a fleeting second he contemplated inviting Clarissa to his house and then they could both go Go-Karting. This thought was interrupted by the conversation he could half-hear in the front hallway.

"What date would that be David?" his mother asked and Tommy could hear her shuffling with the pages of the diary by the telephone. "Only if he wants to, though, I won't make him do anything he's unhappy with. We have to consider his feelings in all of this." There was a pause then, "Yes I know David, but I don't want him to think that we don't want him here. He's my son just as much as he's yours." Tommy's attention was entirely fixed on the telephone conversation now. "I'm sorry, I know you don't mean that. Let's just see what he says. I won't just pass him over and he has to come home, I can't bear to be without him forever. We'll speak again tomorrow, goodbye." And the receiver was replaced.

His mother returned to the room and both Brandon

and Tommy looked at her inquisitively. There was a long pause as she went and sat in her favourite chair.

"Tommy." They waited with bated breath. "That was your father." Again the silence. "He wanted to know if you would like to go back to The Manor at Christmas to see Clarissa." There was a very long pause as Tommy tried to take this in and then he spoke.

"Would you be comfortable with that?" he asked, thinking he had used very grown up words to hide a very prickly situation. Why did all this pressure have to be on him? There was another pause and he knew that his Mum and Brandon were exchanging glances. He wished he could read their minds. Why hadn't one of his powers from Fliw been that he could read people's minds in this world? His mother nodded gently and he looked at Brandon.

"Whatever you want to do Tommy," Brandon said. "Your Mum and I would like you to come away for a while with us to Florida in the summer holidays. We know that it's not fair for you to miss out on seeing your Dad." Tommy felt like someone had punched him in the stomach. Where had he been for the last week? He had tried desperately not to take sides in this situation and somehow it was all out of his hands. He had come to like his new step-mother and he even, almost liked but couldn't say so, his step-sister. Now he had a new potential step-father and he couldn't find anything to dislike about him either.

"I don't want to talk about this," was Tommy's feeble attempt at a response. His mother went out to prepare the evening meal and Brandon helped him to set up his new computer game.

Tommy felt like he had been transported to a different world than the one he had left on Friday from school.

Nothing was the same as when he had left it, and he was completely disoriented.

After dinner the three of them sat together in the front room and Brandon asked about what had happened whilst Tommy had been at The Manor.

"Are you sure you want to ask? I thought you would want to ignore them." Brandon and Tommy's Mum both smiled slightly, his Mum spoke first.

"Tommy, you're allowed to enjoy yourself. You have to agree it's better than when Daddy and I weren't happy?" Tommy nodded.

"OK. If I told you half of what had happened you wouldn't believe me."

"Well just try us," challenged Brandon. Tommy started to tell them about his adventures, but he could tell that they were just smiling and nodding. Eventually he gave up and said,

"I'm absolutely exhausted Mum, but you have to believe that I am an Arch-Druid and that I have to go back to solve the quest." His mother nodded patiently.

"Of course you do dear, and Brandon and I will make sure that you have some days at The Manor at Christmas. Now go and brush your teeth and get into bed." With that she got up and went into the kitchen.

Tommy went and quickly washed and then cleaned his teeth. The house felt familiar and he could not wait to get back into his own bed. As he padded softly along the landing the telephone rang again and he heard his mother's side of the conversation.

"Yes David, he told us something similar himself." Tommy crouched at the top of the stairs and listened. "No. I don't know what's behind it at all, but if it means that they are content to be together and they don't fight, I don't see any problem do you?" The conversation went on for a little while and Tommy sat at the top of the stairs with his knees tucked up to his chin. Soon the conversation ended and the receiver was replaced. Tommy suddenly felt the urge to ask what had happened and he quickly went downstairs.

"Mum?"

"Yes dear?"

"What's happened?"

"Nothing dear, come and sit for a while." Tommy went into the front room and he and Brandon listened whilst his mother explained how David had told her of Clarissa's story about strange happenings at the Manor House. Tommy listened and nodded every time he agreed with Clarissa's account of something. His mother was not particularly worried about this and she extended a question to Tommy.

"Do you know anything about this Tommy? David seems to think that you have made Clarissa believe your daydreams. What do you think?" Tommy weighed this for a while and then shook his head.

"How could this be a daydream Mum? Everything I have dreamed and everyone that has been involved had an explanation for what happened. If you really think that there are things such as fairies and goblins then you're just as bewitched as I am." All three of them smiled and nodded, Tommy took his cue and went to bed. As he lay in the darkness of his room he contemplated the feasibility of Hoy-Paloy and his adventures in The Kingdom. Was it possible that he had seen him in broad daylight behind the two girls?

He had too many thoughts swirling in his head, but eventually Tommy fell into a deep and dreamless sleep. He was however content in the knowledge that he would have a chance to prove or disprove the theory at Christmas.